Thinker

And More Unusual Tales

Mike Gutowski

Oddity Odysseys

Cover artwork created by free AI
Narrative Consultant: Philip Beckmann

For permission requests, contact the publisher, at:
Email: dadx3g@msn.com
Facebook: @mike.gutowski.62

softcover ISBN: 979-8-9873433-6-4
eBook ISBN: 979-8-9873433-7-1

Printed in the United States of America

Science Fiction, Dystopian Fantasy, Poetry

First Edition

Table of Contents

Introduction

Consequential dreamers dream they are dreaming. Nonsensical dreamers dream they are consequential.

In the annals of human known history, many mysteries remain unsolved. One look at the night sky has mesmerized the creatures below it since creatures have existed on this tiny planet orb. The highest level of species creatures named it Earth. More questions than answers have evolved about the meaning and purpose of it all.

Certainty about many aspects of existence seems a near ungraspable absolute. At the basic creature level, survival methods have been learned, but sustainability requires further exploration and extrapolation of facts and accurate conclusions. Unfortunately, humans allow into their fact orations fuzzy truths.

Many outer space objects have entered the earth's atmosphere and fallen into the lands and waters all around the planet. Many objects have been found and identified. One specific lifeform, previously unknown and not yet classified in the biological and anthropological earth records, recently entered a human controlled neighborhood.

An identity of this creature has yet to be confirmed. And now, our first Unusual Tale unfolds.

THINKER

Storyboard:

Characters:

Thinker/Sitter: the mysterious alleged extra-terrestrial confounding the minds of human politicians, citizens, and all creatures around it.

Little girl/Emmy: a pre-teen aged human of quite high intelligence level, possibly a genealogical member of an off earth world civilization.

Narrator: Independent voice transitioning scenes.

News Reporter: human writer employed by the Dundalk Eagle, a community newspaper.

News Services: other news organizations operating in or near the community.

Politicians: corrupt plotters and greed-mongers subjugating the humans they socially and politically control.

Civil Service workers: police, military, government construction workers.

Other humans: criminal drug gangs and their members; local inhabitants.

Religion Members and Leaders: members of churches living in or near the community where Thinker/Sitter visits to observe human interactions, including religious Elders who manage the church communities.

Scene: a typical metropolis.

The Bus Stop Bench Sitter

Conformity causes death of the human spirit. Here's how societal control works, tempus est dominus.

Spout a false or fictitious tenet, either at universities, or media outlets, or tech organizations intent on capturing, imprisoning, and molding like putty the minds of the populace.

Market the tenet, using the above indicated allies.

Market loud and long and hard, until the general public begins to believe the tenet as truth, regardless of the facts which become buried under the feet stomps of the gullible.

Recruit followers, especially organized media, into the fold, crease the fold so the subjects of the subjugation methods can't escape the crazed crowd now primed to utilize the tenet as a communications weapon.

Unleash the crowd's voice upon the populace.

The crowd will then make the rules and create methods of subjugation under the watchful eyes of the original false tenet minders.

Why does this tenet subjugation method work?

Because the people who want to fit into society become blinded about how society is crafted and molded. They close their eyes and minds. They gladly accept such an organizational premise. Accepting subjugation and the subsequent pain induced by not following along, suffering pain such as intellectual and personal isolation, cancellation of sentient communications, banishment from society are the tortures imposed by the tenet masters.

The goal of the tenet makers is to destroy tradition. They know tradition is a conglomeration of wisdom, which too includes egregious falsehoods amidst the recipe bowl, in the ingredients usually used for so long they are assumed necessary ... tempore en dominus.

Is there such a thing as a single-source energy concept? That is, whether a singular source emits all that is and all that there ever will be? Is the source controlled, or is it the infinite controller? Is it sentient or is it an accident? How does something evolve from nothing? Exploration further needed, always needed, infinitely needed.

Perhaps infinity can best be defined as a circle. There is no starting point and no end point, just a series of circuits about the course, over and over again. None of us individually have an infinity of time to figure out exactly what infinity is, and that circumstance is infinity's best defense of intricate discovery, prevents dissection and exact explanation, like black holes and alternate dimensions, a good rain helps the thinker. Eventually, it is realized that infinity is a prison.

There is science in such thoughts. Grains of sand create a defensive beachhead from the long dead sea life generated by loose detritus. An elevated level of positive ions influence. There exists also iron in the irony system.

There are many masks, like the weather, cloaking an ultimate solution. Maybe the stoic Greek philosopher, Epictetus, had it figured right. A planetary world is a big pie, of many ingredients. The pie serves all inhabitants of life forms many, to determine the worth of a taste of it. Sometimes the pie maker claims a secret ingredient for success of the taste menagerie. Don McLean's "American Pie" song is practically a prayer about life's follies and the fools marching along or sitting back with their feet up, even those who secret themselves away from such raucous parties.

The music is a prayer of fate and fall. There is Aerosmith's "Dream On", as stoic as is gets in musical communication. Everyone is looking for their piece of the pie, even scientists. They have no magic black Top hat which causes their perspective bias object to appear, disappear, and reappear in another space.

Two words illustrate the point like a sword thrusted true into the human heart. Climate change. Today's intellectual pie. Tomorrow's "Green Eggs And Ham".

But I digress needfully. The background tale of a forthcoming story serves as a pie plate. From voids spring life. Any circumstance emanating from the void is possible, thinkable, credible, incredible.

Examples are numerous, such as "The Divine Number"; radio signal bursts from FRB121102 where somewhere in the universe is the origin; Dodecahedron universe shape suppositions and consequences; ancient Sumerians math system based on twelves and sixties (5x12); Anunnaki humanoids born of 6 fingers on each hand and 6 toes on each foot; an Amazon Brazilian tribe born with 12 fingers, 12 toes (a congenital condition), polydactyly is a birth defect affecting one in 100 thousand people; music organizational construction of 12 notes, 12 tones, octave 12 steps; see also Einstein's string theory; the universe may have 12 fundamental particles.

Greek mathematicians in 535 BC created designs for the stars and the night skies. Pythagoras believed he discovered a sacred code of the universe, then termed it as music of the spheres.

B. Heim and Stephen Hawking developed a 12-dimensional theory.

In the Religion realm sphere, examples also abound. Catholicism: 12 Apostles, after Judas committed suicide, a new one found, Mattias. Hindu: 12 Chakras; Islam: 12 Imams; Judaism: 12 Tribes.

In government politics world, Majestic 12 was formed by U.S.A President Truman to investigate whether extra-terrestrials existed and whether potential contact was possible or feasible.

As reported by the <u>Dundalk Eagle</u> (a small local newspaper located just outside the city line):

"Understanding music of earth life existence strains the minds of many societies. Perhaps we are a soulless bunch, we humans. Such a thought was ignited by my investigation of the story I am about to portray for the reader. I shall convey to you, as best I can, an odyssey of a being who sat on a bus stop bench one day, and never left it, although some street stories say this being left the bus stop to hide behind the walls of an invisible bubble. There is little evidence to suggest such a reality. Only word of mouth, and such a communication system moves like a slug, traveling in circles until the circle's expansion bursts, or shrinks and crushes itself. Lies become truth. Truth becomes nonsense.

I will leave it out there in the realm of media publications for collective introspection to interpret and mine further for any nuggets of truth, veracity, or otherwise human perceptions ultimately determined. The very concept of the story is elusive, hides in the shadows, as if discovery is not the goal. For discovery can become a curse, one where interpretations and perspectives become skewed based upon prior conceptions and misconceptions, biases, even wants and needs. Perspectives spectacles can crack, break, fog the mind.

We all seek to find what we want, but spend not enough time in determination of what it is we individually, and then collectively, need. I am not a scientist. In a way, I abhor their method of thinking, as it has evolved into a religion, full of dogma-like mantras, full of dogma. Retributions flow wild from such a banal starting point.

The least noble of thoughts and actions start from the same point as the most noble. It is the path they traverse, and the course they take which predicates the vortex of their influences and infections spread. Humans are no different than viruses, and subject to the same worldly existence hazards of defects.

Whether the story is about us, or the abandoned bus stop bench sitter, remains a question. Perhaps it, he, or she was comfortable when taking a seat at the bus stop, not to travel, but to rest. A pleasant space in some way unknown to others.

My perspective, as a citizen and independent reporter of such activities, and truthfully, urged onward by my own economic and social needs, remained noble yet selfish in that I craved fame and financial recompense in order to find a place of rest for myself, a solemn domain of comfort, and a space curative of my own indiscretions brought onto my being as the usual and many viruses both biological in nature, and formative in educational indoctrination.

Such diseases are known rampant in every society of humans, in every dimension, all the way down to the smallest microbe.

Talk about the neighborhood, the bus stop infrequent usage by neighbors, then abandonment of the neighborhood by local citizens and government leaders, then the bench seat became more useful from the sitter's life perspective.

I prefer the viewpoint of the abandoned bus stop as either the starting point of another universe black hole or a comfortable place to sit for those in need of a seat. Mindful reflection has the potential for meaningful speculation. Or soothing inflection. Is it time for earth to become consumed? Has the sitter been sent to earth from another place or dimension to take an account of earth planet necessity in the solar system? Or has the sitter merely come to observe the human condition, how it works and doesn't work in a society of billions, cut up into community sizes of thousands. Many thousands, of no single mindset or purpose.

The novelty of the bus stop and sitter winds a course

in the media minds until a comfortably numb ignorance reigns, until one day, the story changes, as a child disappears, then another, then nearby residents and politicians of faux noble minds and evil inclinations.

From my sources I will continue updates of this story for the remainder of my assignment to cover it."

A child walked by, stopped, accompanied by friends, pointed at the still perched upon the bus stop bench sitter.

"There it is, the thing that sees, but we can't see it see. It sees on its own. In secret, in the open, into us. It changes us, but we can't see how, until we act."

"You're crazy," one of the friends suggested.

"You'll see. Maybe not now, but someday, somehow."

The group laughed loud in falsetto voices of the very young.

<u>Dundalk Eagle</u>, Sitter update:

"Sitter is the story of a man, presumably, who sits on a sidewalk bench at a bus stop that almost no one uses, and the city wants him to move so they can tear down the bus stop location. Citizen perspective of the sitter changes depending on the viewer, modified by the changing elements such as modern-day society, culture, media viewpoints, from glorification, rebel, hero to denigrations, terrorist, sinner. Or is it (sitter) a babysitter? Stalker? Mocker by virtue of his very existence? Does sitter ever communicate in words?

Sometimes passersby start to see it move, but perhaps they are mistaken, seeing what they want to see. Some say they hear it, mimicking the sounds of birds, and the neighborhood, and creaking buildings, and the wind in the trees. Some believe it is a god. Some believe it is a thief, come to steal virtue and ideas. And the media is claimed by the public at large as the worst transgressor, creating sitter into anything that feeds their thirst for attention.

The politicians are next to worst, turning sitter into a threat to their power, casting aspersions of little evidentiary substance, creating evidence that doesn't exist in a reality created by the politicians and their lackeys. Military potential was ignited too, as a means to institute an aggression protection scheme. Was the sitter a threat on a larger scale?

No creature needs to justify their existence. No creature molded and created themselves. Once the existence opportunity arrives, the vessel of existence, through learning and experience, self-determines their fate. The purpose of sitter remained a mystery.

Such a mystery has been interpreted as a threat to the physical surroundings of the bus stop bench.

At this stage of my reporting, sitter exists unmovable, in physical or emotional respects. HE IS MERELY THERE, IN THAT PLACE. And because sitter is in that place, others want to take it away from him, make it theirs, plunder control, or protection, or erect verbally or by law a symbol for their inner desires, wants, needs, however nefarious or noble those desires emanate forth. In effect, sitter is merely a mirror reflection . . . of them."

Time passes. Never stops for the human-made street signs. A tension in the community begins to arise as steady as the sun rises and sets over the sky horizon boundaries. It seems those boundaries have been breached in unexpected ways and means. Amongst the population, speculations and miserations each develop a mind of their own making.

<u>Dundalk Eagle</u>:

"Update: The sitter has disappeared. The neighbors don't know when, why, or how. The story as of today continues. Some of the stories I tried to get printed were not accepted by my Editor as they were lacking witness source names, and thus, difficult to confirm for publication. You shoot for the moon and sometimes hit just a nearby satellite.

One story involved a drug gang shootout, and witnesses who did not wish to be named, gave incredible stories of how the bullets from each weapon ricocheted off of the spot around a nearby space the sitter is believed now to occupy. The space is bordered by a housing project and a government building. The sitter wasn't seen there, but witnesses believe he has concealed himself in some unknown manner because they hear noises emanating from the space, usually in the evenings.

During the drug gang shootout, bullets apparently struck the empty space and some of the bullets ricocheted and struck the drug dealers themselves. Two different gangs were shooting it out, and all of the members eventually died, but before so, the police reports indicate each drug gang member was killed by the very bullets that were projected from their own guns, as if the entire affair was a massive suicide encounter. No bullets were found to have struck the buildings.

The police offered no explanation for fired bullets that physically turned around and struck each gang member who fired a gun. The witnesses were adamant about what they had seen, but the police thought perhaps the witnesses, under stress, misinterpreted what they had seen. Humans can't see the travel trajectory of a fired bullet.

I visited and interviewed some of the residents. Some of them, although a bit drug addled at the time, confirmed the stories which I had read from the police report written narratives. I was unable to contact the witnesses interviewed by responding police because the police report blocked out their names. Not sure why the names were blocked out."

The local area churches seemed concerned about community relations between citizens and police given withholding of information in the police and local media reports. A curiosity arose regarding the lack of politician responses concerning the gang shootings in the neighborhood. The churches banded together to begin their own investigation.

<u>Dundalk Eagle</u>:

"Update: Churches full of people came forth one Sunday, to observe and pray nearby Sitters mysterious alleged place. Some of the Pastors decided, as a matter of safety, to draw a red chalk line around the space now deemed to be 'Sitters' place. The chalk line helped warn church members to not walk too close towards the place of 'Sitter', a name now adopted by the local community. The line formed a circle around the supposed invisible spot. Some of the adults reached over the line and felt nothing, just air.

On one later visit by a Church children's choir, the children were heard to be talking about a thinker in the invisible bubble space, as marked by the red line circle. When asked about what they saw, it was described as a glowing person, maybe a man, seated on a barely visible bench with his elbow on one knee and his hand propping up his chin, motionless like a statue. They earnestly sang some Church hymns towards the red circle. Afterwards, the children were heard wondering about this place of a 'Thinker', the children's name for the occupier of the red-lined space. I suppose it is a Dr. Seussian type of name, but a name seemed required for journalistic integrity to take hold. Adults continued to call the apparition 'Sitter', but the children's imagination inclined them to call it 'Thinker'.

Nothing happened, except in the imaginations of the adults and the children, but their descriptions of what they viewed became well known to the community. The imaginings were reported as miracles in some Church newsletters, but the Church hierarchy dismissed the idea. Speculation abounded long and loud enough for some varied Churches and Religious Orders to select elders for the purpose of making visits to the red-lined space. Weekly reports were made available in a mini-newspaper available free on Sundays. I attended many of these services, then recruited members to send me a copy.

The local politicians in a larger local newspaper began publishing weekly reports, not wanting to miss out on an opportunity to publicize the need for a subscription to their work product. The larger newspaper initially published reports mocking the idea of a bus stop sitter influencing a community in a positive way. The byline read 'Nothing To See Here, The Story of Sitter'. But the believers thought otherwise long and loud enough for the moments of the Sitter's presence to enter local legends lore. The local citizens still called him Thinker."

<u>Dundalk Eagle</u>:

"Update: my previously rejected story referring to the initial appearance of Sitter seated for a lengthy time on a bus stop bench has now been authorized for release to the public. See the report below.

'Cops came to remove the bus stop sitter, but he-she-it doesn't speak, or look at them, almost as if a statue. They tried to touch him, but couldn't as there was some sort of electric type force field around him. Local scientists were interviewed, requesting their names not be used, to pose a theory that in reality, the bus stop sitter is an inter-dimensional being, resting, but in that dimension rest perhaps takes many years, sometimes generations, to regenerate health. What ill health may have occurred is not certain. Such a long sitting posture for earth humans is not recommended.'

Updates pending."

Neighborhood Revitalization

After the above-mentioned reports, a revitalization of the neighborhood is proposed by the local politicians. Local politicians encourage their constituents to visit the Thinker location and initially ask him to leave. Some of them do so but no movement occurs. They then shout at him to get up and walk away but fail to convince him. He remains steadfastly placid in demeanor.

Then, a local press campaign is initiated, prompted by local politician requests. False stories about the Thinker abound in regular intervals both in newspapers and TV affiliates. A psychologist and a scientist provided opinions which are shown on local media stations and reported in newspapers saying that Thinker could be considered a menace or danger to the community.

"The current situation for Thinker remains uncertain as all around him, buildings are slowly being torn down in a part of the neighborhood that had been abandoned long ago by local residents due to poor and unsafe conditions. The reason local politicians neglected it and let it rot is a question they will not specifically answer, but now there is money to be had by them, it seems, so they've turned Sitter/Thinker into the boogeyman to get what they want. A resolution to remove Sitter/Thinker has not been identified. It seems the politicians hope it will merely wither away if in fact it actually exists."

The city condemns the land upon which the housing project building occupies, then issues plans to tear down the housing project building with intent of creating condominiums for luxury housing, but when the hired workers start deconstruction, varied accidents happen, workers are injured as their tools break, construction materials burn unexpectedly, or rust quickly and crumble.

The military is called to determine if some type of weapon has been hidden there, they try to cordon off the area and study it, but similar mishaps occur, as if the area is cursed. They begin to experiment to determine how extensive is a contamination caused, allegedly, by the now mythical being known as Sitter/Thinker.

Strange things happen, in sounds, to creatures like rats, mice, birds, insects even. University scientists are hired to investigate, run tests, and issue findings merely speculative.

The Thinker seems to have protection around it, either created by itself or by another entity or perhaps it is controlling the environment around it for protection, including control over the animal and insect creatures, as if the turf is now the Thinker's place, and can be shared with other creatures at its discretion.

The politicians are livid. The real estate developers are livid. The citizen investors are livid, as they all would profit from such Revitalization.

<u>Dundalk Eagle</u>:

"The politicians, developers, and investors don't seem to have a real grasp of the situation in Thinker's realm of existence. Psychologists and scientists can't seem to fathom a purpose or need for his presence. It is rumored by some in the community that people working in the government Administration are suddenly disappearing. Perhaps, this circumstance is a means of not further denigrating themselves in the eyes of the public. But truly disappearing? That seems a stretch of reason."

The average citizen knows that to trust any government or government officials is suicide. The government gets what it asks for in its own back yard.

Little girl, a church member and singer in the choir, visited the invisible dome. She wanted to ask questions of Thinker. She concentrated on his presence until she heard a voice sound.

Thinker: Humans wear invisible perception glasses. Sometimes their glasses become hopelessly fogged.

Little girl: I don't understand. Did you like our singing?

Thinker: This place needs more work than an old blind dog with three legs. Yes, a beautiful sound.

Little girl: All of us are trying to adapt to the changes.

Thinker: This universe is a godless wasteland of zero emotions, dedicated to consumption of all things it encounters, whether now or eons from now. All other concepts serve as distractions from the known yet unaccepted horrors. But perhaps one future day, your descendants will discover and acknowledge this truth, then learn a better technological means to survive such chaos.

Little girl: I don't understand. I've been taught otherwise.

Thinker: There's a fine line between sensical and nonsensical, and that line has been long ago erased.

Little girl: Are you saying humans are now trapped in Schrodinger's cat box and the cat's name is Catch-22?

Thinker: I'm stunned by this question.

Little girl: Why?

Thinker: Wait. … I checked memory bandwidth for such a concept. Found it, digested it, then formed a response. Your species lives on the cusp of a time when the nations of this world will once again ignite a philosophical renaissance. Unfortunately, quite a few nations are afflicted with asinine perspectives, then spew forth bullshit. Not sure what is bullshit meaning, but I know what is shit. You seem concerned.

Little girl: Do you mean we put the shit before the bull?

Thinker: Yes … that's it.

Little girl: So, these nations want their fair share of the shit.

Thinker: Yes, so to speak.

Little girl: Explains a lot. Are cities and towns demanding the same . . . shit.

Thinker: Yes.

Little girl: Some humans are quite stupid.

Thinker: Yes. Some. My research shows Stupid as the number one major study in many high schools and colleges around this world.

Little girl: What's the next most studied major?

Thinker: Philosophy, even though it is disguised by the name of Humanities Studies.

Little girl: What are those?

Thinker: Thinking methods of exploring how to live in communities. Literature, Philosophy, History, Languages, Arts.

Little girl: Nothingness flows through and around all times and spaces. It should be added to the Periodic Table of Elements as Atomic number zero.

Thinker: Science. A different study topic. I wonder about your genealogical history.

Little girl: I have to go now, but just wondering if dark matter accounts for 27 percent of the universes' total mass energy. I read dark matter is hypothetical. Then there's the place of dark matter. It was nice communicating with you today.

Thinker: Yes. Thought, and thought, and thought, then thought some more. Time is a cruel teacher.

<u>The Dundalk Eagle:</u>

"Today's news is light on content, so I thought I'd explore more of the Sitter/Thinker story, which now has evolved into a 3rd person's involvement who will remain anonymous. And no, I'm not the 3rd person. The local politicians got together this past weekend and formed a circle around the invisible bubble, at least parts of it, and spouted out a crudely written poetic diatribe, ostensibly for attention. Here it is:

'So long, farewell. I'll see you another day. In a dream, or spell, as remembrance of the walk away. As the autumn leaves construe, on these knees during the drift breeze's way. Too many times, we tell of hue's dancing lonely rhymes, during taunts of memory blues.'

And that's that, on off back to their corrupt houses of politics and homes of deceit. We, the citizens, know who to blame. We always know who to blame whether righteously or not. We exist as the edge of dawn and spawn of blame."

Here's the kind of world we live in today. Apologies are not worth shit. Don't forget to flush. Astral projection is either myth or science, but not both. A politician who steals from citizens should get a swift trial and a death penalty sentence. Tariffs mean you can have this product but only if you grossly overpay for it. Love while you can. Too late is not replaceable."

Thinker wonders about the little girl he rescued on the playground. He tells her, during a subsequent meeting of minds, "Once you see death you can never unsee it". "I've seen death", she responds, "when my goldfish died". Thinker responds, "It is much worse a sight than the moment you saw, in many cases. A shout you cannot hear, a scream you cannot here, from a fish. The human or other land animal can die loud, and emits ugly sounds. Scary sounds." Little girl asks, "Are there other kinds of deaths besides silent deaths and noisy deaths?" Thinker says, "There are unknown deaths of unknown causes and known deaths of known causes and known deaths of unknown causes. That's about it. All of them become forgotten deaths over the course of time." Little girl added, "And forgotten lives as well". Thinker responds, "I'm only here to observe and record, and sometimes to advise from my mind." Little girl wondered, then asked, "Do you put thoughts in my mind." After a bit of silence, little girl walked away and back to the tasks of daily routine.

Sitter Thinker then paused to negotiate a ponder with himself. May have to undo what his observation near the bust stop caused to happen. The drug dealer was affected, permitted local newspaper stories to be published and evolve into mythical mysteries. Such mysteries can spurn dangerous speculations amongst the local citizens. Thinker's superiors warned about such types of interactions. One day in the long distant future, their living dimensions may be security compromised.

Thinker reviewed his earth observation experiences to date. Some seemed to have a significant influence on his perspective interpretations. During the first gun shooting incident the little girl was knocked down while her choir group fled. When she got up she noticed another friend had fallen, shot in on leg. The little girl helped her choir friend move away from the scene but then each was shot at again and the friend a second time and little girl a first time.

Thinker had been watching from inside the dome shield. Thinker reached out from the shield wall and pulled each little girl into the dome. The friend little girl was critically injured and died. The little girl survived. Thinker nursed her back to a healthy status. The little girl was very sad about her friend's death.

Thinker thought about this situation. Wondered if his presence had become a pre-sage to these events resulting in the friend little girl's death. Still, Thinker realized two choices now existed. Each would violate his observation rules, and he had already broken the intervention rule when attempting a rescue of the two little girls. Thinkers' mind advised to intervene.

The choice happened freely if not instinctively. Cryo-freeze the dead little girl, temporarily.

The other option was to reverse time and save the life of both little girls. Such actions would again violate the observation only rules. Interventions could change world and universe history for all of time. A time reversal had only happened once in universe history, and the causer of the incident created a retraction of universe expansion which led to a popping open of numerous black holes. The causer was immediately executed by the overseers of that dimension. Thinker analyzed the time reversal potential results considered and learned the bullets ejected by drug gang members would have struck numerous other choir little girls at the scene, killing many of them. This option was not feasible as it resulted in more deaths.

Thinker than pondered whether a shadow bend miasma should be used. A shadow bend allowed Thinker to split the body from the mind. The body and soul would separate. The body would remain in stasis inside the dome shield, and the mind would inhabit the shadow and become visible only as a shadow impenetrable by objects. Such methods are allowed to be used to achieve better observation points and perspectives. The shadow mind was often used to gain knowledge.

If Thinker used the shadow mind option, permitted by his work protocols, then he could rescue the entire group of innocent choir members from harm. Still, the impact of such actions on the time scale could not accurately be measured, so this option opportunity must remain dormant in the present time. Thinker determined a use for it in the future without abandoning it as an option.

Eventually, the drug gang returned with more numbers of humans carrying more weapons of destruction. Thinker's shadow companion self-confronted them and offered advice.

"Comply or die."

An immediate response from the gang echoed throughout the neighborhood. Bullets sprayed out from their weapons into the shadow body. The shadow body dodged and darted every attempt of a bullet to strike. The gang members where then greeted by the ricochet of the bullets directly back towards them as bullets rebounded from impacts against the dome shield. Within a matter of minutes, most of the drug gang posse lay dead or dying on the ground.

The leader of the drug gang became enraged, and ordered a direct hit upon the dome shield. The order was executed, and the projectile ricocheted off the dome and back towards the remaining gang members and their leader, finishing the death dealings of the day. A calm silence remained, at least until the local politicians took to the newspaper reporters' stage and railed against the dome inhabitant.

Thinker's shadow returned to the dome. He spoke to little girl.

Thinker: Little one. Listen to me. In this hour of horrors, they who want to control you have failed in their mission. They will not stop. You must choose your fate. I suggest it be to not let them take away the who that is you.

Little girl: Okay … okay.

Thinker: Remember. Always remember.

<u>The Dundalk Eagle:</u>

"Local citizens are buzzing with the news of the drug gang activity recently. Many of the gang members were killed or badly maimed during an altercation of unknown origin. Neighborhood witnesses recited baffling stories of shots fired at no particular targets for unknown reasons. Some speculated they just decided to practice their aim, or just blew off steam for no apparent reason. The big mystery is how did these thugs actually die. Bullets seemingly from fired from nowhere mowed down the murderous gang members. Oddly, the local politicians didn't seem bothered by this incident except to declare a mourning period for family members of the deceased."

All of a sudden, the politicians are searching for light amidst their own circle of lies and deceits and financial corruptions. The citizens see it. The media outlets see it, but they each fear speaking out because the taxation gun is always loaded in politician holsters. They are theft machines. Who hasn't had a superficial relationship with a washing machine exterior as it vibrates during the rinse cycle?

All that can be pleased are pleased. All that can't accept such a life are expected to shut up and get out of the way. For the younger citizens, they attend schools politically directed to propagandize reality, not how to think but what to think. For students, any deviation is crushed by grade or detention penalties. Schools have become living breathing, soul crushing monsters.

Still, silent resistors abound. They communicate in whispers and small get togethers so as not to trip the paranoia wires of their elders. Little girl grew up amidst this miasma of human chaos. Thinker wondered if she had yet to make a choice. All is poison in this world, Thinker deduced. It is amazing there are still some who resist the chaos mind virus. Perhaps they were born calm, unfazed by the chaos wheel crushing all on the false propagandized side.

All manners of civilizations have been born, raised, declined, and died. Civilizations of humans have become compartmentalized by physical borders of land and seas, and by cultural, social, and political borders of those who have the power delegated by the elders. No civilization escapes such a life setup of structure either physical, intellectual, or spiritual.

Little girl: How come you don't blink your eyes?

Thinker: I do blink. Just not that often.

Little girl: How does that work?

Thinker: The outer portion of my eyes are protected by fluid that absorbs the dust until it . . . disappears.

Thinker noticed little girl imagining a means to understand.

Thinker: You can't always control what happens to you, but you can always control how you react to it.

Little girl: Like my birth?

Thinker: A human concept is that birth of a child is a miracle. It isn't. It's more so the biological result instituted by sexual relations, either of flesh or chemical processes medically induced. What happens after those first moments, post birth, is when and where the miracle, so to speak, begins to occur, as a reincarnation of the gene mix of male and female past interactions genetically, over many earth years. After birth, the child learns how to us the physicality of itself, but eventually, the mind can take over the thinking process allowing the human to grow in knowledge.

Little girl: So, if one fidgets their life away, they will miss out on the potentials of the biological life living in it.

Little girl: I have more questions.

Thinker: Go on.

Little girl: Why do politicians continue to punish us for our successes? They seem to change the rules to make it more difficult to succeed.

Thinker: The politicians are afraid of citizen power, especially the power of independence.

Little girl: What is independence? I have heard the word, but the politicians seem afraid of it.

Thinker: Politicians are afraid the citizens won't need them any longer. Perhaps it is what some doctors call psychologists, humans who study how the mind thinks about using certain words and how it can be warped by unusual humans.

Little girl wanted more information to consider but Thinker could see she looked tired, perhaps hungry for some food, so he made a joke.

Thinker: If a submarine is a sub sandwich diving into ocean water, then is a poopmarine a turd diving into a toilet?

Little girl: Your humor needs mending.

They laughed.

<u>The Dundalk Eagle:</u>

"Every writer writes to portray a reality or a fantasy derived from a reality with extreme prejudice. If humans could create a weapon of mini tornados or hurricanes full of sand pebbles, then they could better protect themselves from harms targeting them. You can't sensibly tether the future if you can't sensibly navigate the present.

A famous author, James Baldwin, advised 'We can disagree and still love each other, unless your disagreement is rooted in my oppression and denial of my humanity and right to exist.' A famous philosopher, Seneca, wondered then advised 'What progress have I made? I have begun to be a friend to myself.'

Which leads me to fathom the following. Any political party seeking total control of the populace they serve is in no way democratic, no matter how much and loudly they claim to be. Such inane thoughts as otherwise deserves no response. It's the painted wall demanding a further painting, then further, then further. They don't know the done of spending money. The smell of done after cooking a meal is one of life's precious satisfactions, yet, the politicians are never satisfied.

The politicians make life a prison sentence. The prisoner must find the keys and escape such a perspective.

Given there exists 7 plus billion humans on planet earth, it is a given that smart people have become a dime a dozen in numbers and quality. Everyone and everything dies. Immortality is a lame fiction. Even the universe agrees.

Humans are grossly outnumbered in this world by creatures of land, air, sea, outer space, and microscopic habitats. If these non-humans ever figure it out, act as one, then we humans are doomed.

The most disappointing aspect of humanity is that too many humans don't desire to exercise their brains often enough. It's so much easier to be just told what to do and how to do it. No questions, no doubts, just do the tasks, then relax and enjoy as much entertainment as possible. Human accept such a life as a peaceful surrender.

They are perfectly happy to enjoy fancy and frivolous passions rotely, following friends of similar thoughts, family members of agreeable dispositions, or even large committed crowds regardless of intentions. Free will and self-preservation are damned. A life is defined by socially helpful desires. Whims of too much fancy dilute life into an irrelevance of time usage."

Under the invisible dome, Thinker and little girl resume their meditations and incantations about universe existence.

Thinker: It appears much of what humans hear and experience was iterated by in-person word of mouth many years ago, but now it is spouted by paid marketing and media outlets, then re-spouted by word of mouth or computer communication methods.

Little girl: Yes. There is much agreement without debate.

Thinker: What do humans say about subjection to this newest communication system?

Little girl: What is truth or truthfulness becomes a daily question. Our many squabbles revolve around what is truth. Perspective is used as a crutch, but the viability of that crutch is often questioned. From physical reality to perceived reality, all is often questioned, tested, rewired in the brain, over and over again.

Thinker: Truth is a deception too often. It can change with the wind of societal norms in quite perverse ways.

Little girl: Yes. A constant struggle, sometimes to the death.

Thinker: Truth is a logic hammer swinging down upon propaganda rails. Gladiators dueling for a true justice. A base human quality.

Little girl: Challenge! We sail in cloudy skies, in virgin born lies, never to sway again, on broken promise ties.

Thinker: Accepted! A fish in water feels at home. A fish in a bowl swims alone. Such can life be, when the fates are unable to see, where a life may flee, except for a bit or progress sewn.

Little girl: The path is long, the path is hard, breaking up into little shards, sounding out many songs.

Thinker: A ring on a finger binds a moment to memories of a bond friendly.

Little girl: The passage of time binds moments to memories.

Thinker: Memories bend as time rends.

Little girl: Are we humans entertainment for you in the same way we are entertainment for the politicians we choose to rule us? It seems we are merely pawned lines in a Picasso painting.

Thinker: Does a grain of sand over time and weather become a pebble, then a stone, then a mountain?

Little girl: Fertilizing the mind with thoughts like mulch assisting the ground to carry forth a little phase of plant life from seed to plant or flower.

Thinker: Depending on the rains as they lay upon the plains of sands and mountains.

Little girl: An apology is an atonement moment necessary to align past regrettable moments with a necessary current resurrection of a wiser self.

Thinker: Rarer than a grain of sand.

Little girl: Much like truth.

Thinker: Truth lay bare everywhere, yet no one can find it there.

Little girl: Lies lay there, yet no challenge dares.

Thinker doesn't respond.

Little girl: What are you doing?

Thinker: Checking my mind box to find rhyming words and magic phrases.

Little girl: Magic?

Thinker: Yes. The place in the mind where wizards dwell.

Little girl: Yes! Yes! Do tell!

Thinker: Well, sort of like magic. Word mixes needed to bake my poetry cake.

<u>The Dundalk Eagle:</u>

"How is it that sometimes life seems too easy and sometimes life seems too hard? It's like mowing the lawn and redoing it again too soon. A mow is a mow is a mow, but the grass is obsessed with growing. A lack of permanency is an exploitation of time's fair usage. Existence was painted with an eternal brush dipped in indestructible paint pallets and hues.

Cycles of life are painted of blood, sweat, tears, fears, jeers, smears, of multicolored brush strokes, upon realities coarse canvas full of human character personalities and intellectual deviances. Too many complications of colors is the palates norm.

A day never exists of all problems solved. A solved compilation hides many unresolved probabilities. All time is a rush towards solutions and further resolutions. Reality never rests. It exists as a salty pork, a talky parrot, a buzzard ever hungry.

A human mind never rests. It eternally seeks to be mined for golden thoughts, badges of hone and distinction. It will never accept solution or absolution, up to the day of extinction. It is a ticking clock of alarm that can't be shut off.

Satisfaction is a bargain between wants and need; between hunting and greed; a struggle of follow or lead; pitting rake against seed. The known is a too large puzzle of still missing pieces. Perhaps, too much knowledge leaves a bland taste in the brain pot. Playing tab with the wind."

Thinker and little girl fashioned word salad comparables while tapping into a poetic vein.

Thinker: Echoes. Activists detractivists. The best way to be happy is to be happy with oneself. Figure out who you are and want to be, what you want to be, and find a way to be you, to be you.

Little girl: Listen. Analyze the sounds human or otherwise. Respond in a respectful way. All of nature deserves respect, and a wariness awareness.

Thinker: Oxymealons. Nothing like a good slice of pizza. What is a good slice of pizza is imminently debatable, as are all matters of taste, whether it be food, drink, clothing, or anything subject to the emotional inclinations of the beholder imbiber. Imbibe the view, the scene, the words, the preen, sounds of hounds, squeaks of geese, grogs of frogs, bleats of sheep.

Little girl: Dictatorships are broken economic gyrations. They start tainted and end fainting.

Thinker: Governmental dead zones. The last vestiges of government monetary control must die the martyrs death, although false martyrs they would be. Eliminate political sausage.

Little girl: A refreshing dose of self-conscious debate. Sausage spoils, eventually. After an extensive conversation amidst me, myself, and I, a consensus was agreed upon that there exists no pie in the sky.

Thinker: A refreshing dose of common sense. The less money that goes to politicians, the more money remains in the control of taxpayers.

Little girl: A refreshing dose of street sense. When citizens trust gang bangers more than the community police force, that's called corrupted stupid. Of course, sometimes the police force is on the side of the gang bangers. Judges, too. Crazy world.

Thinker: When all is lost, much can be found.

Little girl: What is that called?

Thinker: Hope.

Little girl: Fate.

Thinker: Taking care of business.

Little girl: A whiter shade of pale.

Thinker: Do the hustle.

Little girl: Undo the bustle.

Thinker: Making dare of pleasure.

Little girl: A darker wade of stale.

Thinker: Best of my love.

Little girl: Worst of my hate.

Thinker: Backwards and forwards.

Little girl: Inside and outside.

Thinker: Emotions.

Little girl: Logic.

Thinker: Tips and gyps.

Little girl: Swindle and pendle.

Thinker: Jack and Jill.

Little girl: Solsbury Hill.

Thinker: What day is it?

Little girl: What night is it?

Thinker: Many suns.

Little girl: More daughters.

Thinker: Dawn.

Little girl: Fawn.

Thinker: Set in stone.

Little girl: Painted in bone.

Thinker: Reeling in the years.

Little girl: Steeling in the fears.

Thinker: Vibes.

Little girl: Jibes.

Thinker: Rock steady.

Little girl: Lock ready.

Thinker: Low rider.

Little girl: Bow strider.

Thinker: Wild world.

Little girl: Cats in the cradle.

Thinker: Jokers wild.

Little girl: Kings child.

Thinker: Walk this way.

Little girl: Talk that say.

Thinker: Reminiscing.

Little girl: Missing.

Thinker: Risk.

Little girl: Tisk.

Thinker: Bask.

Little girl: Task.

Thinker: Gun.

Little girl: Run.

Thinker: I see.

Little girl: I feel.

Thinker: Do you feel like I do?

Little girl: Lights, I feel.

Thinker: Can you feel dark?

Little girl: Yes.

Thinker: May I test you?

Little girl: Yes.

Thinker: What time of day is it, outside this dome?

Little girl: Time of day? In what part of this world?

Thinker was taken aback. How could she know the time anywhere in this world? Thinker amended the question.

Thinker: What place am I thinking, then what time is it there?

Little girl: My mind will go around in circles until it spots the place where you wish me to see. You don't have to tell me the place name or coordinates. Just think it. Oh, there. Okay. Here's my answer.

Thinker could hear her answer in mind.

Thinker: Correct. How did you arrive at answer?

Little girl: All I do is analyze the question and the possible answers. My mind seems to work like a map, reading the surface of any object. Did you know rocks have names? And animals, too? We speak different languages, but my mind is able to decipher the sounds and find meaning in them. I thought everyone could do that.

Thinker: I see.

She is so much like us, from my world, Thinker thought. Quite amazing.

Little girl smiled a knowing smile.

The Dundalk Eagle:

"I used to believe in Fate. Not so much anymore, yet, Fate will have a say on any given day. If someone has a bruiseable ego then that ego is too soft. When we each stopped believing in each other, then the relationship was over.

The major media are mainly a branch of dumbass bastards and caddy bitches play acting as journalists and broadcasters. Words sometimes get in the way of making sense. Most of the media challenges sense and advocates chaos. Citizens risk their lives to save lives. Politicians threaten lives to fatten their bank accounts and investment portfolios.

Searched my imagination to discern Thinker's possible self-reflections about what he has seen and experienced thus far. Here's what would seem apparent. Why do they talk in riddles? That's how they make sense. It doesn't make sense to my ears of years. The ears hear. The brain interprets, sometimes wrongly. Sometimes the brain is unable to manufacture a meaning from the extant word usages.

A word is like a brick. Once it is laid down as a structure of meaning, it either persists or is stress challenged. Pointing out the obvious is obvious. Pointing out the controversial is controversial. Little bumble bee, why do you hover upon the porch roof's edge? Are you playing a game? I see a younger friend of yours. I hear the buzzing sounds and feel them bumping against my eardrums. Playful laughter or work dedication? Or merely exercise for wings and mandibles? Fun it is to observe such sporting exercises. All thought has a purpose."

Thinker continued to explore Little girl's cognitive capabilities.

Thinker: Passion sometimes overtakes sensibility and breaks it into little pieces.

Little girl: Does the soul think?

Once again, Little girl sent Thinker down another path of humanity exploration.

Thinker: Versatility is a vision. Humans attempt versatility as a mind quality, but seem unable to maintain a logic path.

Little girl: Did my soul question cause your mind to wonder?

Thinker: Perhaps we should travel another path together.

Little girl: Okay.

Thinker: What are those creatures?

Little girl: Where? I can't see through the cloud fog.

Thinker: Pardon me. Here, I've opened a window in the fog for you to see.

Little girl: Squirrels. Have you never seen one?

Thinker: Well, yes, a few times, but thought they were cleaning bots.

Little girl: Bots?

Thinker: Yes, bots. They remove detritus.

Little girl: How?

Thinker: By consuming it. Like one of your planets sea sponges.

Little girl: Sea sponges are not bots. My mind latched onto the word bots. Now I recall reading about them in a science book. They are machines.

Thinker: Perhaps we misunderstand each other. All creatures are bots where I come from.

Little girl: Are you a bot?

Thinker thought about this classification system for a bit, then a bit longer than a bit.

Thinker: In my culture, you are a bot.

Little girl: If I'm a bot, and the squirrel is a bot, and all creatures are bots, and all of life down to the smallest particle is a bot, then we've all been created and programmed as bots, even you. Perhaps the universe is just one big bot maker.

Thinker: Perhaps I should become a bot, to better understand what it is like to function as one.

Little girl: Yes. You can fantasize you are one, and then emulate bots you've observed.

Thinker: To assess viability and purpose for myself as part of my task here.

Little girl smiled.

Little girl: Oh! I would like to know how a squirrel thinks and what it thinks.

Thinker nodded.

Thinker: Let the transformation begin.

Little girl: I would so much like to play like them.

Thinker paused once more. The value of thoughts hinges on expressions of them in words.

Thinker: I need you here to observe, take notes into your mind. Your perspective will help enhance my perspective.

Little girl: Sounds like fun.

Thinker thought, "Yes, fun. What is fun like?"

His body remained inside the dome, but his shadow-self entered the human physical reality. The squirrels would only see the shadow, but their other senses may be able to detect another living presence. The squirrels were only 100 feet away from him, but they stopped a bit, one by one, to give him the side-eye look, which is their natural body structure ability. They remained chewing while observing. The detritus was actually food sources such as bits of corn, crawling insects, and more.

Thinker noticed a garbage bin up against one of the nearby walkways leading up to a building's rear entrance. A lid of the garbage bin was open. One or two squirrels hopped down from the bin, clutching food bits in their mouths such as bread, lettuce, french fry strands. They paused as the shadow approached, gave it a glance, then continued along.

Thinkers previous observations recalled humans walking along with paper bags containing food, then they would sit down somewhere, reach into the bag, and pull out circular slices harboring dark colored patties and oozing of red globs of liquid, sometimes too yellow globs and green flat orbs. Smaller bags of food from the larger bags contained french fries. Finally, a liquid drink of varied colors was pulled from the bag in a thick, circular, papered cup topped by a plastic lid like a trashcan lid in appearance, then a thin plastic tub was plunged into it. This type of eating seemed a bit ritualistic to Thinker. The eating ritual had apparently become a natural human trait over time, known by many of them.

Thinker deduced no difference in these human ritualistic tendencies when comparing them to the squirrels eating systems. Lots of chewing, side eyes glancing to check who was watching nearby, assessing any potential threats waiting or approaching.

Thinkers shadow returned into the shield dome.

Thinker: What do you think?

Little girl: It seemed the squirrels knew you were there, not just your shadow. They recognized you were not one of them, but they sensed no threat and went along with their daily business.

Thinker: What is their daily business?

Little girl: It is to find food, eat it for nourishment, then carry some away to safely store some of it for future use. They didn't seem as playful. Just their mannerisms, quick, keenly aware, displayed a sense of happiness and satisfaction. To them, work is fun and useful for survival.

Thinker: They don't smile. How do you know they are happy?

Little girl: Finding food and sharing it seems to give them happiness. The little ones seem energetic and playful, some chasing each other round.

Thinker: Ah! I didn't notice. Thanks for mentioning that observation.

Thinker then wondered if his cultures leaders would appreciate such knowledge gleaned.

Thinker: It seems, based on my research and experiences here that some humans rule over their language uses during shared verbalization moments, and some allow the society to rule over their language uses and thoughts verbalizations.

Little girl: My reading shows that many civilizations follow a similar cultural path.

Thinker: Can you provide an example of your conclusions?

Little girl: Yes. Let's suppose a human male is walking down a street sidewalk while chewing bubble gum, and also reaching into his shirt pocket and pulled out a folded piece of paper, while his shoes are unlaced, the shoe string flopping around on the concrete, and while his head is topped by headphone speakers covering both ears. Suddenly, another person on the street sidewalk shouts, "Stop!". Why did the other person shout to stop?

Thinker: During my observations of humans doing the very same thing, I can make some guesses as to why the other human shouted to stop, such as the bubble gum chewing was annoying to those on the street, or the second mentioned assumed the first human reached into his own shirt pocket to pull out a folded paper with directions written on it, but the second human wanted to offer directions, or the second human thought the first human was going to pull out a handkerchief to blow his own nose and the second human thought that possibility was disgusting, the second human shouted to alert the first human that his own untied shoelaces might cause a stumble, or the second human could hear the first human's speaker headphones because the volume was turned up so loud the second human didn't appreciate annoying sounds coming out of the headphones, or the traffic light up ahead had changed and crossing into the street could be dangerous at that moment. Many other possibilities exist.

Little girl: Yes. Perhaps the first human had regularly walked the sidewalk many times and knew it so well he felt comfortable not paying much attention, so a lack of his attention during this specific moment became usual. There was a bus lane up ahead at the street intersection where the bus stopped to pick up passengers. The second human didn't know the first human so didn't know the first human would not cross there.

Thinker: What about the handkerchief, stumbling potential, and loud music sounds?

Little girl: Thinker distractions.

They mutually laughed.

Thinker: I've noticed that music has a melody that sometimes sounds like a laugh.

Little girl: The tones of spoken words help to create music, but I suppose anyone can try to sing, yet the emanated sounds may not be heard happily. The proper pitch and tone may exude sadness, joy, apathy, and many more emotions. Even music without words can evoke these emotional sounds. Does your world have music?

Thinker: Yes, although it sounds like cracking ice fields.

<u>Dundalk Eagle:</u>

"Random thoughts during these uncertain times flow wildly, sometimes softly. Specific words are used for specific tasks in social, work, and religious venues. Feeble minds are often bored. Remember the good times. Let the bad times fall away. Saving yourself will earn a thank you. Let yourself be alone. Contemplation time is pleased by sound silence. Cursed by another human's romantic love inclinations isn't vile, but it is incredibly distracting.

Mind you mind. No one else will. Possessed by mind spirits is a crazy karma. Mind your mind! Think this way! Ha-ha! Just go away, cantankerous spirits!

Haunting thoughts of stupidity moments ravish the mind, crushing good memories in the process. I wish for myself not to dream while asleep. A silent blackness sponges the soul of nascent thoughts. Any spark of mentality ignition drains the energy of the sleep engine production. Ugh!

Tenpins Art: 'That's just great' verbally spewed sarcastically means 'not great' at all. Like when the echoed roll of a tenpins ball down finely waxed lanes cracks the cream-colored pins into a spattering and noisy mess of chaos, while a single pin remains standing alone as the din deflates into a dead silence mirroring the mind punch. Together, the single standing pin and the receding chaos rule supreme. Managing enjoyment is difficult. Managing chaos is enlightening for mind, body, and soul."

Thinker wondered why little girl sometimes prefaced her thoughts using the words "my dad says". Perhaps she harbored some reservations about her dad's meaning. Sometimes when she said "my dad says" her emotional means of expression displayed an eloquent embrace of her dad's words, repeating them like a poetic sonnet.

Little girl: Are you god?

Thinker: No.

Little girl: Then who are you?

Thinker: Someone who cares.

Little girl: Cares? About what?

Thinker: . . . Let not the dark praise our presence, for in daylight we offer presents.

Little girl: Time to sleep off the dread of too many words in my head.

Thinker: Let's fix that. Perhaps my sin is a visit uninvited.

Little girl: Every sentient human commits sins. Oddly, as if a curse bestowed upon us by the gods, this subconscious, we punish ourselves to equal the balance scales.

Thinker: For the balance scales, it is. The universe is an equal opportunity killer. It bears no concept of humanity. Such inclinations are born of ignorance, generally acting child-like, unaware of consequences.

Little girl: You speak of metabiology.

Thinker: Yes. An algorithm of immense power and ignorance.

Little girl: Such a creation can only pursue expansion and totalitarian control.

Thinker: Merciless control. Or in human-like terms, cult-like dominance and dominion.

Little girl: It almost seems like there exists no purpose involved.

Thinker: Yes. Only existence, by any means, in any manner, shape, or form.

Little girl: An engine of doom?

Thinker: Depends on where you exist.

Little girl: Walking in madness, whether eyes open or closed, whether body asleep or awake. An addiction not different from that of a drug abuser.

Thinker: Humans are obsessed with death. Would be better if they were obsessed with life.

<u>Dundalk Eagle:</u>

"Everything should be grand here, but it isn't. Time is a bend. The past is almost never completely accepted. The present remains unexpected. The future remains a trickster, remains a mysterious mystery, sometimes crushes all proposed plans. Think, believe, dream, dare. A better life beckons. Hear the call. Don't stall. Abandon failure fears or drown in tears.

Enlightenment helps darkness to fade away. Filters through knowledge cracks. Need to observe the features of life in the face of a human. Stark details of form. Nuances of thought exuding from the eyes. The soul tickling of sounds. Emotions vibrations. We walk masked. Sometimes that mask remains impenetrable, of purpose. Who needs to know us, anyway? We are mere dust rolling off the universe shelf.

By the creators restrictive necessity, reason unknown, we can only deduce that a curious reality exists. We seek to know more than the reality and physicality of earth life. Our existence meaning is relevant. A mirth myth clings to us, murky as it seems. Recovery from the despair of not knowing must be allowed to float away into the mist of unresolved emotions.

Our children have been Orwellianed. Humans are the only creatures able to comprehend the greater madness all around us. There is a magic to the touch of observation. It allows us to extrapolate an expansive meaning attributed to existence purpose. Our children must learn to master this madness and harness in the net of common sense.

Pollutions of perceptions regularly stains the human mindset. Choking on truth can be overcome with a slap on the back. Truth isn't fickle. The people who claim to speak it are."

Little girl: What does "one true" god mean?

Thinker: It is a saying posited to demonstrate that the speaker is wise enough to know there is only one god.

Little girl: So, is there a god?

Thinker: I've never met one. In my civilizations record, there is no direct reference to evidence of a god.

Little girl: Why do my family and friends believe in a god?

Thinker: You would have to ask them.

Little girl: I've heard them asked by others. Unhappiness results. I've concluded there is no true evidence of a god. Just symbols like statues and paintings.

Thinker: Well, some humans like to think there is a god to alleviate their stresses of taking responsibility. When failing or faltering in character, demeanor, and actions, they say "it is god's will".

Little girl: I know. I find that a bit childish. Blaming others for their own mistakes.

Thinker: If it is any consolation, of the many places I've visited, the same circumstances exist in this regard.

Little girl: Blaming others is better than blaming themselves. Again, childish.

Thinker: I tend to think of life from a mirror view. Teeth brushing and mouth gargling moments. A hand towel serves as an editing tool.

Little girl: Bathrooms are a good thinking place.

Thinker: Your politicians seem to have a different view. If they don't like the way things are going, then they would rather burn those things that impede their intentions.

Little girl: My dad says half-baked is half edible.

Thinker: I've noticed. Inflation, riots. Over and over again.

Little girl: I would think the citizens would have learned by now that their elected politicians are not good people.

Thinker: I've noticed. They treat citizens like slaves. Are all cities and towns like this?

Little girl: No.

Thinker: I must study these circumstances further.

Little girl: My dad says in a truly free society we must suffer both geniuses and half-wits.

Thinker: Who controls the god controls the society.

Little girl: Bad things happen in those types of societies.

Thinker: I'm sure.

Little girl: Wishing it were not so.

<u>Dundalk Eagle:</u>

"Local scientists have been trying to construct a concept of how to judge Thinker's presence here on earth. Their analysis of the reported stories of witness accounts lead to several conclusions.

Thinker can't be touched by any object on earth because it is not all here. It resides in mini-space dimensions: one for the body, likely in the nearly invisible dome, and one in shadows, and one in a quasi-physical status which can recoil in response to physical contact attempts from humans and other animals. In effect, it can dodge bullets.

All creatures exist as a grand illusions orchestrated by the viruses that reside within them. The most precious resource in this world is time. A creature not requiring regular rest can better use time. Time never rests.

If we are creatures of time, then we've been mugged by our own weaknesses. We are time stuck."

Thinker and little girl continue their ruminations. For them it is koan time. Paradoxical discussions where answers to problems take the form of questions, stories, or riddles. A bending of phrases helps to cleanse the mind. Much like placing a damp soul over an outdoor clothesline. Let the wind blow soft and steady until time finishes the chore.

Thinker: Never allow yourself to become a prisoner of you own wants. Such a condition tends to evolve into many painful experiences that deteriorate the soul.

Little girl: Discriminating against anyone is akin to discriminating against oneself.

Thinker: Warring against war is war.

Little girl: A great unresolved mystery of life revolves around one question. Why does life exist?

Thinker: Hailing a cab is a Nazi salute. Newborn babies are genderless. Politicians steal from us for our own benefit. The major media has lost its mind.

Little girl: Persuasion about healthy facts becomes a sickly puke.

Thinker: What should be, isn't. What shouldn't be, is.

Little girl: The poor remain poor if they don't strive to be more.

Thinker: Adaptaman. A human who can adapt quickly to any condition or circumstance.

Little girl: The unknown is a fortune of undiscovered knowledge.

Thinker: Shadows are weapons of mass reduction.

Little girl: Good one. This world is infested by goons. The goons want everyone to become goons. Their loneliness drives such a mind vehicle junker. The highways are riddled with junkers that pop and stop as klunkers.

Thinker: Innocence is lost when poor thinkers defrost.

Little girl: Romance quality isn't measured in quantity.

Thinker: Every space could use a little more in size or a little less in filler.

Little girl: Washings slowly destroy cloth threads just as caring slowly destroys emotion treads.

Thinker: Do best what you do.

Little girl: Destruction is a creative stew of chaos and added spices.

Thinker: Choose those spices wisely.

Little girl: Spoiled food either by cooking or wasting bends time into a blob gob.

Thinker: Wants are destructors of needs if not properly tended.

Little girl: Incompetence and corruption have regularly seeped into and eventually dismantled every civilization on this rock planet.

<u>Dundalk Eagle:</u>

"When the government rules with an iron fist mentality, then a sentient cleansing becomes a necessity. Their education systems have morphed into institutional ideocracy. Promises of hope but impositions of systematic chaos persist. To die fat, lazy, and whiney is not a graduation goal.

The government steals through taxation. A curse that fills the government purse. Nonsense outweighs sense in their every communication.

Happiness comes from how life is lived. A mind bereft of thoughts is like an empty can of coffee grounds. 'Why' remains the biggest and least logical answered question in every community. The best way to not see the details of any artwork is to look only at the big picture.

Truth isn't fickle. The people who claim to speak it are. People have a reason to care depending on what values they cherish most. Religion is a hell of getting stuck with idiots. Neither such god or human exists or existed. The shortest way to any destination is to not take it. Taxing the mind is an expensive proposition. Humans are obsessed with death. Would be better if they were obsessed with life.

When we free ourselves from the expectations of others, then a sentient calm mind resides in winds balms. Statistics are a math way to say 'go to hell'. Years ago, getting lucky meant not running out of car gasoline on the way to work.

Politicians are foolish and not fooling anyone, just paying the fools to follow them. Like dogs, the politics world leaders lick their own butts regularly, at least when seen publicly playing out their own miseries. In the game of life, rules breakers abound. The crux of any story hides among nuances. To be a guest of your own life is a sad way to travel along. The essence of a corrupt political party is their insistence that not believing their word is a crime requiring punishment. Many minds tangled.

Using lies to debunk truth is the essence of evil's ugly intent."

The issue of how human people view and describe each other arises by chance. Thinker and little girl describe each other, and each is surprised by the descriptions. A common bond ensues. Each doesn't know their true parents. In Thinker's world such discussions rarely occur.

Little girl: You look almost human.

Thinker: I'm stunned.

Little girl: I meant it as a compliment.

Thinker: Nonsense outweighs sense in everyday human communications. I see you have questions.

Little girl: Happiness comes from how life is lived.

Thinker: Is our communication now a word off?

Little girl: I'm ready.

Thinker: You first.

Little girl: A mind bereft of thought is like an empty coffee can.

Thinker: I'm trying to picture it. What is a coffee can?

Little girl: A place where coffee is stored. A small space place.

Thinker: Like a horse stall?

Little girl: Smaller. You can't carry a horse stall.

Thinker: Don't be so sure.

Little girl: The issue of how humans perceive each other arises. They regularly seem surprised, socially, in a new environment space.

Thinker: Perhaps they are lost.

Little girl: Perhaps you are lost.

Thinker: In a way, we are all lost.

Little girl: Who is we?

Thinker: I suppose an answer depends on the philosophy of life followed.

Little girl: On many thinks. How a person looks in appearance. How they speak or otherwise communicate. Their temperament when doing so.

Thinker: Masks, you indicate.

Little girl: Yes.

Thinker: In my world we don't communicate behind masks.

Little girl: Why not?

Thinker: Because masks are not necessarily temporal in nature. They are for effect.

Little girl: Like to play along. For show.

Thinker: Yes.

Little girl: You look almost human.

Thinker: Again, what a surprising thought.

Little girl: Your shadow self seems like a mask.

Thinker: I suppose it is. It can influence an object or creature physically. It morphs the reality experience. The perceiver then must quickly seek an explanation, thus becoming temporarily blinded to the moment's significance and how or whether to respond.

Little girl: A powerful temporary blinder, it is.

Thinker: Humans see in frames. Each frame blocks out much thinking perspective. Shadows can see multiple frames at once, filter through the frames, and quickly make a response judgment.

Little girl: I want to learn how to better control my shadow self. A bully at school taunted me and my shadow self suddenly appeared. It scared each of us. The bully fainted.

Thinker: Just one shadow?

Little girl: Many shadows.

Thinker: How many?

Little girl: Don't know. I almost fainted, too.

Thinker: You seem to be a rare species of human.

Little girl: Is that good?

Thinker: Good and bad. Human emotions and perspectives tend to induce exploitation of such gifts for good and bad purposes.

Little girl: Can you help me control the shadows?

Thinker: Worth a try. We will see whether reality is awake for the task.

Little girl: Shall we continue the word off?

Thinker: If you wish.

Little girl: Zen is a means of lying to oneself to assuage the mistakes made while abiding those lies.

Thinker: We lie to ourselves as a means to make the shame of coping with existence bearable.

Little girl: That's god sense.

Thinker: Ah! You left out an 'o' in good. Now we are getting somewhere.

Little girl: No, I didn't. There are no gods residing in this universe, just humans who pretend to know them.

Thinker: Have you visited the entire universe?

Little girl: No. Have you?

Thinker: No, but parts of it. I would not assume a god or gods control the universe, but I would not presume there are none.

Little girl: I understand.

Thinker: When my civilization first discovered this world you call earth, we thought of it as humans would think of a dust mop. Moving around all of the viruses that inhabit all life. The viruses play with and against all places. They inhabit all soils, all oceans, all creatures. They promote life and they take it away.

Little girl: And they are not gods.

Thinker: Time to rest these minds of ours.

<u>Dundalk Eagle</u>:

"Anytown is a place where the shit in peoples' heads is excreted onto the streets outside. This city and surroundings is quickly becoming such a place. Or I should say, becoming worse by the day. The many citizens who have escaped likely will never think they miss this place. All dreams of success have vanished. The politicians won't allow it except for their own benefit.

The remaining population consists of politicians, their associates, and citizens striving to sustain themselves without the means to leave. The invisible dome remains. Unshaken. But for how long?"

Little girl: I missed you.

Thinker: I was out shadowing the city.

Little girl: What do you think?

Thinker: Unusual variety of lifestyles. Some parts vibrant. Some parts abandoned.

Little girl: It has always been that way, my daddy says.

Thinker: Odd.

Little girl: How odd?

Thinker: Where I originated, useless space is a crime against the soul.

Little girl: I don't understand.

Thinker: We are of one soul, but not of one mind. If we were of one mind, then our world would die.

Little girl: So, many minds and thoughts improve life?

Thinker: Yes, in our experience.

Little girl: My daddy says the dregs of society don't live on city streets. They live in the homes of the elites.

Thinker: Environment is the only god wherever it may exist, and all living creatures serve as servants to it. Daylight and night light rule over every time cycle. The gods would not heed any creatures if they were lonely.

Little girl: To be lonely is a choice that acts like a habit. That habit can be broken and tossed away if the lonely person decides. A beautiful transition.

Thinker: Beauty tempers the human mind. Dangers abound. Persistence in helpful tasks are required.

Little girl: As humans, our mind drifts.

Thinker: To drift is a freedom dangerous if uncontrolled. Humans collect objects of memory to hide themselves from an accumulation of mistakes.

Little girl: Yes, we adapt like any other creature, but emotions tend to get in the way.

Thinker: Planned and proper intentions must be carefully considered.

Little girl: What is the biggest distractor of good intentions?

Thinker: Religion. It offers a noble course, but humans often fail during the implementation phases.

Little girl: We learn from our mistakes or fail if we don't learn. That has always been our way. Flip flops clack in our minds.

Thinker: It is quite obvious what has happened to human societies on this planet. A significant number of them qualify as certifiably unstable or mercilessly corrupted by selfish emotions and deeds. Those afflicted in each society endlessly persecute those who are not like them. Morality has been flipped on its head. The crazy and corrupt become divine and the honest and moral are treated as enemies of the immoral society. Your world in a nutshell.

Little girl: Too many eat those nuts. Trust in the media is shattered. Perspective is paid for by the highest bidder. Facts have become an inconvenience. Charismatic leaders and entertainers can manipulate and control the minds of millions and billions of people.

Thinker: True. But the people themselves are capable of making sentient decisions, despite all of the negative soup tossing.

Little girl: What is negative for some is positive for others.

Thinker: Pants pooping wanna be's who never wanna do. Earth language synonym, whiners.

Little girl: Ha, ha! We call them politicians!

Thinker: I would amend your thought as follows. Not just politicians, but also the people who claim to believe in them.

Little girl: You said people instead of humans.

Thinker: Yes. I'm adapting my language while here.

Little girl: One can analyze every situation properly, and still circumstances can change on the fly. Variances of facts and lies can arrive randomly while life and living introduce continuous changes into the existence equation.

Thinker: In your ancient times, the physical weapon symbolized a display of potential rage. The wielder of the weapon supplied the emotions to express rage. A need to eat. A want to suppress. A bow and arrow, a gun and bullets. Steel machines rolling on land, floating houses movable on and under oceans, metal birds in the air and above earth. Explosible objects large. A continued exploitation of more modern weapons resulted in global mass destruction possibilities.

Little girl: Self-defense is a human right. Citizens merely attempted a means to assert self-defense rights, not just through word usage, but also through weapons usage. It is difficult to feel safe anywhere. Non-human creatures of the land and sea also have weapons and armor in their anatomy, and create boundaries using sounds or constructed barriers and traps. It is possible that humans learned to hunt and defend themselves by observing methods used by the animals in their environment.

Thinker: I must say, while I was out on my shadow explorations around your city, I observed interesting self-defense methods at use by little animal creatures and human creatures. Protective measures. A keen wariness in the face and amidst body movements. Even amongst children.

"Sometimes dreams want to get in the way of reality. Don't let them. Remember to live the reality or risk losing it forever.

No one is entitled to a savior. Save yourself.

During life's living, the mind tries to bury the bad times and encourage the good times to rise up regularly. Lessons are learned during each of these moments. These learnings must be resolved in the present to help prevent further trips and falls."

Thinker noticed Little girl seemed weary.

Thinker: What's troubling you?

Little girl: Nothing. We are talking a lot. And nothing is changing. Yes?

Thinker: But a lot is changing. Just my being here has changed a lot here. The politicians are scared. The more they speak to the public, the more they reveal their true motivations. The more they expose their true selves.

Little girl: How so?

Thinker: They've exposed their capacity to lie. The citizens have noticed the lies, and they are tired of hearing them.

Little girl: Humans who can't handle the truth invent lies.

Thinker: Now you understand. Further, many civilizations throughout this universe, for political reasons, have invented gods to cope with what they don't understand. Understanding the ways of how sentient life exists is a simple process.

Little girl: Don't you want to know the origin of sentient life?

Thinker: No. It is an unanswerable pursuit. A conjecture involving much thought but revealing no answer. What is the point?

Little girl: Comfort.

Thinker: Comfort is a temporary condition. We have never found it to be a permanent condition. Comfort is a temptation to no longer learn. It is a condition antithetical to continued existence and learning. Existence either advances or steadily decays. Decay is inevitable. The purpose of all living things is to exist, learn, adapt, and further a species or living entity down the last atom of space. There is no fiction without reality but there are many realities without fiction.

Little girl: I see it both ways. Each feeding the other.

Thinker: An interesting thought.

Little girl: Each living thing serves a purpose, and this purpose is intricately connected.

Thinker: An unbreakable truth. Good observation.

Little girl: There are some who do not seek truth. It binds them.

Thinker: Yes. Some seek the perfect scheme to acquire wealth.

Little girl: And many do not see. Ignorant of the truth. Perhaps they don't want truth.

Thinker: Truth hurts.

Little girl: I wish for a perfect day.

Thinker: To have a perfect day would mean the end of all things good.

Little girl: Why?

Thinker: No further significant energy needs to be exerted when that happens. The mindset starts to enter a downward spiral. Good would gradually lose meaning while those satisfied with good will slowly decline for lake of desire.

Little girl: So, drop a penny and let it ride a gravity wave to add a touch of imperfect. Then, invite another perfect day to arise in the future. Repeated penny drops are necessary.

Thinker: Even after problems are resolved, a fear of repeating the same mistakes can sometimes rattle the mind.

Little girl: Do you make mistakes?

Thinker: No.

Little girl: I make mistakes frequently. That' how I ended up her with you.

Thinker: Funny.

Little girl: I'm laughing inside.

Thinker: I can almost hear it.

<u>Dundalk Eagle:</u>

"Just came over the rumor mill a report of further unusual activity in the area of the invisible dome. A new security guard was assigned to work at one of the nearly vacant buildings. Some neighborhood residents have heard and seen the guard acting strangely.

He walks rounds in the building and around the outside to monitor for any squatters present, and whether they pose a danger. Somone spray painted a sign on one side of the building. It reads, 'Beware! Don't Wake Guard Until Daylight'.

Of course, the guard's purpose is to stay awake at night to monitor activity inside and around the building. Some remaining residents believe the guard has a medical condition that causes epileptic fits. Would explain an erratic leaning walking posture, the sudden stops as if frozen, then sudden frantic touching of the bricks on the building searching for something not visible while whispering.

When the guard's shift ends, just after dawn, the guard's walking gate seems perfectly fine. Walks tall, appears physically fit. No residents were able to draw a connection to the invisible dome."

Thinker notices little girl isn't in her usual dome spot. He searches for her. She walks towards him.

Thinker: Find anything interesting?

Little girl: Just walking and thinking.

Thinker: Anything you can share?

Little girl: Every living creature emanates energy. This energy emits chemical signals towards all creatures nearby. Some react positively and some react negatively.

Thinker: How do you judge the reactions?

Little girl: Well, an odd reaction would be displayed by sounds and body movements.

Thinker: What do you mean odd?

Little girl: Not normal.

Thinker: What is normal for any creature encounter may vary.

Little girl: Okay. Maybe I can learn about specific creatures and how they react to each encounter.

Thinker: The balance in nature can be altered by many event shifts. A typical imbalance occurs when familiar noise levels are disturbed. A balanced, safe sound level mitigates the possibility of dangerous or manic shifts. Some wail loudly. Some fall silent. Either alteration serves as a warning.

Little girl: Is this imbalance permanent? Can it be altered?

Thinker: Circles within circles desire no end. Proof that life seeks no ending.

Little girl: Death remains an expected occurrence whether imbalance is accepted or not.

Thinker: Yes. The hardest part about the living is the learning.

Little girl: With great power comes an imbalance favoring corruption and subjugation.

Thinker: Yes. But the imbalance can be equalized. A calm and patient mind stimulates rational thoughts and imaginations. Soul seedings stimulate growth of beautiful bounties of flowers and food thoughts.

Little girl: Many fields of beautiful bounties.

Thinker: Hopeful yields of blooming sentience.

Little girl: Still, it would seem there is some hell to pay for simple pleasures.

Thinker: Many places to go. Many truths to perceive. Much to give. Much to grieve.

Little girl: A breath of fresh air is often needed.

Thinker: Memory can feed that need. Time works a way backwards to catch a glimpse of relevant moments. These retentions reveal hints of present progressions and possible future events.

Little girl: The mind seeks solace. The body seeks rest. The soul seeks peace. A cognitive triumvirate.

Thinker: I must say, your mind works better than most humans three times your age.

Little girl: I didn't notice. Thank you.

Thinker: One brain. Three mindsets. Beautiful.

Little girl: Is all life this way?

Thinker: Across the known universe, no.

Little girl: Is that a good circumstance?

Thinker: Sometimes yes. Sometimes no. If the mind controls the brain, then the mindset is better able to evolve towards multiple perspectives.

Little girl: Is that a good circumstance?

Thinker: Again, sometimes yes. Sometimes no.

Little girl: Perhaps an example, whether good or bad.

Thinker: Let's take earth humans as an example. Once the human entity appeared on this planet, after 4 billion years of evolutionary history changes, they developed into the fastest evolution of the mind in all known universe history. The explanation is the resources available in this planetary system which humans call the solar system.

Little girl: I must think more about that. Learn more about it.

Thinker: A noble and necessary pursuit. Cultures tend to kill themselves from within.

Little girl: Our scientists believe they can solve all of this world's problems.

Thinker: Boasting, they are. Correct, they aren't. This planet is still hiding many mysteries.

<u>Dundalk Eagle</u>

"On Human Reason Sentience: Here's a simple and understandable reason reminder to help those conflicted by religion theory: humans create gods; humans create governments. These diabolical titans have clashed since the beginning of sentient creature existence.

On Time Stamps: Too long can sometimes be a matter of seconds.

On Living Rules: In order to seize the day, one must use the body and mind regularly. To do less is a flirtation with death.

On Writing Jerky: I often think I have nothing else to write, but then interaction with life around me convinces otherwise.

On Stimulus Reminders: I've often been reminded of why never to give up when looking at the object of thought stimulators collected over time, such as gifts, awards, rewards, collections, and books.

On God Fakes: How long before we have AI generated gods?

On Empty Moments: When I was homeless, a wardrobe wasn't my thing.

On Mind Clogs: Snow often reminds of nonsense, from tiny tidbits of thoughts to large blobs of fakery.

On Problem Resolutions: A quick and permanent solution to any problem is preferred.

On Nature's Way: Snow exudes from natural elements in a way similar to human body farts. Silent but deadly in spirit.

On Fictions: Perfect is a human mind invention. No one and no thing and no science is perfect. The concept is an escape route from reality.

On Broken Promises: Politicians promise Paradise and deliver rat holes.

On Sentience Defined: Many humans prefer a safe, happy, peaceful existence but it is difficult to subsist amidst whiners and buttheads.

On Useful Exposures: It's times like these when we come to realize just how many useful idiots exist in every society. Spawned from the bowels of educators and media outlets, the weeds of propaganda overcome the fragrant flowers scents."

Little girl: Just some more thoughts perhaps needing further clarification.

Thinker: Go on.

Little girl: The evacuation of human bodily fluids is necessitated as means to cleanse all human sensations of the numerous rigors of existence.

Thinker: As humans would say, that's a can of worms your mind has opened.

Little girl: So, I thought something good.

Thinker: Yes. Useful good. Your interest implies questions about how humans have existed on this planet. Let me pose a contrast.

Little girl: Okay.

Thinker: On my world, our bodies are replenished internally, after breathing the air of the environment around us. Regardless of the location of existence, our bodies automatically adapt and permit usage of needed elements, and reject those not needed. Human's on earth have not yet developed such an automatic, intelligent, biological separation system suitable to all earth environments.

Little girl: A lot for my mind to swallow.

Thinker: We don't consume swallows.

Little girl laughed.

Thinker: Unfortunately, earth's governmental systems exploit control of the resources needed for humans to survive, then parcel the usage of these resources in methods they deem fair.

Little girl: Explains why so many humans are barely subsisting, and a small percentage of humans are hoarding large amounts of resources. Giving the governments more money causes our own survival problems.

Thinker: As your writer's and author's would say, 'That's life'.

Little girl: You left out what the philosophers would say.

Thinker: You must learn that information yourself, then question it for the rest of your life. Make adjustments along the way.

Little girl: The path is long and the instructions even longer.

Thinker: Such is life.

Little girl: Life becomes clearer when reality becomes more real. My friend Phil told me so.

Thinker: Humans have a unique ability to twist and shape reality into an unrecognizable appearance.

Little girl: Much like Halloween costumes distort the reality of the wearer and perceivers.

Thinker: Yes. What is Halloween?

Little girl: You must discover it!

Thinker: Good one.

<u>Dundalk Eagle:</u>

"Undoing the cheating of cheaters isn't cheating. Let them howl like lonely dogs in the dead of night. 'I miss you' sounds like precious words when listening to street rioters. May they choke on those words. Might juggle their brains into a new realization. 'Don't touch the books. Why? Some of them are haunted. Will give you nightmares.'

The search for what we are looking for never ends, not even in death's bed."

Thinker: Humans have been created as flawed creatures. If gods indeed created such creatures, then what kind of characters are they who made them with so many extant flaws? In what gods can we trust?

Little girl: Maybe the gods destroyed themselves and all of their creations much like human creatures have done to themselves, then scattered about the universe to correct their mistakes, regrouped, and then tried to survive the errors of their arrogance. The human creatures have lived many millennia of years seeking outs a means to correct these mistakes. We are still searching for ways to exist properly on this Earth, while dodging meteors, comets, and asteroids let loose during the god wars. Perhaps the gods are more like us than we are like them.

Thinker: My civilization has been pondering a useful answer to ameliorate such problems, still survive, and seek a better existence path. All things ever entering the existence stage are connected. From first life came many, including crude, simple, and more complex evolutions.

Little girl: Seems human creatures are created robots serving the whims of the gods.

Thinker: Well, we are either test dummies or robotic objects acting out various existence scenarios, not for the benefit of us, but for benefit of them.

Little girl: We have life, however created. We try to do good. Some life has defects.

Thinker: Humans call defects as evil. Some evil is born. Some is developed. Some are in the development stage. Judgments are made along the way.

Little girl: Judgment is provided by unstable people no matter how much grounded and noble they present in appearance. They need to better learn how to objectively judge themselves and others for latching onto a provable fact and reasoned truth. Such personal contentment is utterly more valuable than the biased judgment of others.

Thinker: Comfortably numb is an ambient relaxation swirling in pillows of ambiguity.

Little girl: Relaxing in the chaos.

Thinker: Reminds me of the politicians in any societal structure. Comfortably corrupt.

Little girl: What's the difference between a Democrat and a communist? Nothing.

Thinker: I'm familiar with human political words and actions. Try on this thought. If a citizen votes for a corrupt politician then that citizen has voted for their own swift destruction.

Little girl: Voting for corruption is a suicide pact.

Thinker: I think we are protected by free speech in this world. Of course, free speech is subject to societal reactions.

Little girl: The benefit of free speech is that idiot speakers can betray their own feeble mind in action. Listeners can choose to crush feeble and untruthful words with a common sense verbal hammer response.

Thinker: Or remain silent and let such garbage expressed thoughts blow away into the gutter.

Little girl: Silence is a protective shield.

Thinker: A life lesson best learned early.

Little girl: Stir the pot, expect some splash back.

Thinker: Cities are human zoos where the elected and appointed caretakers play dirty.

Little girl: Is that a general description of opinion or learned experience speaking.

Thinker: A little bit of each.

Little girl: An incredible amalgamation of nepotism and favoritism ingredients.

Thinker: A goulash of greed gone wrong.

Little girl: Fate can be friendly. Fate can be foe. Remain at the ready, when fate makes a go.

Thinker: That's some spicey word stew. Diddy time?

Little girl: When all is lost and none can be found, just turn around and listen for sound.

Thinker: All sounds beg the light for a sight of origin.

Little girl: I want to do, I must be seen, working away at what I mean. To idle is waste unless needs breed haste.

Thinker: Spicey buns.

Little girl: Cinnamon flavored.

Thinker: Is your mind tired yet?

Little girl: I found myself thinking about wandering wonders, origin unknown. The unknown lays upon the soul a heavy burden.

Thinker: No one can truly know you until you know yourself.

Little girl: Lies and truths battle it out in humility fighting matches.

Thinker: Thinking is the engine of acting. Acting is the engine of doing.

Little girl: Success and failure walk the same tightrope.

Thinker: When the Administration branch of any government wields too much power over the financial fate of a civilization, it must remain honest and fair in action. Even a small bit of dishonesty starts an avalanche of citizen misery.

Little girl: Civilization is full of unmarked graves housing monsters and slayers to citizen trust.

Thinker: Many marked graves display civilization traitors.

Little girl: In free and fair government systems the citizens control the government.

Thinker: Many governments forget or ignore such duties of the system. Beware. Many temptations are enchanted by emotions. All of the human senses battle each other for supremacy. Do you understand?

Little girl: Yes. Leave no temptation standing during a pursuit of knowledge. Would you like to know my name?

Thinker: Yes.

Little girl: My name is Emmy.

Thinker: My earth database says the name Emmy is primarily used as a feminine given name and is often a diminutive form of Emily or Emma. From Emily, which originates from the Latin name Aemilia and the Roman family name Aemilius, Emmy carries the meaning "rival" or "imitator", symbolizing ambition, determination, and a desire to excel.

Emmy: Thanks for letting me know.

Thinker: Remember. Temptations can be controlled, correlated, put in a box. Every moment involves a tug of emotions which can be nullified by imagination resolve.

Emmy: Yes. I will remember.

Thinker: Self-reflection is good, but don't allow it to rule supreme or you will end up a couch dreamer.

Emmy: Remember.

Thinker: How does you city continue to exist amongst the death and destruction here?

Emmy: We pray for better. We try to convince the politicians that we expect and need more civility.

Thinker: I see and hear and smell that method isn't working.

Thinker: How long has this city existed?

Emmy: Over 200 years.

Thinker: Unfathomable.

Emmy: What?

Thinker: Excuse my response. Understood.

<u>Dundalk Eagle</u>:

"Rumors persist regarding a confrontation between drug gangs frustrated they have not yet taken control of the area around the invisible sphere. Almost no residents remain living there now since the local government officials have abandoned a restoration

92

plan. It was postponed due to more feasibility studies needed.

In truthful words, it means the politicians have created committees requiring more taxpayer funding, a portion of which will be siphoned back into the politicians bank accounts. The politicians remain riding the invisible sphere, spouting out regularly that all the cities problems past, present and future have been caused by it. Such folly rise the propaganda train of the larger media outlets.

My interviews with citizens tell a different story. Nothing has really changed since the sphere arrived. It merely takes up space like the abandoned buildings take up space. The most relevant question of the moment is what happens next. The drug gangs remain twitchy."

Thinker: This universe is a digestive system that acts just like a human digestive system.

Emmy: What is this universe a digestive system for?

Thinker: The waste of the other universes around it. We are all witnesses to our own lives from origin to demise.

Emmy: Why are you here?

Thinker: I am not here to fix your problems. We are here merely to observe and understand them, the origin cause, and potential solutions. Wait, I sense something approaching the sphere shield. Let's listen.

Drug lord: Who are you to be a judge of our means and methods?

Thinker: I have not judged you. You have judged yourself.

Drug lord: Ping! Ping! Ping! …

Emmy: What was that sound?

Thinker: A man shot at us.

Emmy: Is he still there?

Thinker: No.

Emmy: What happened to him? Did he leave?

Thinker: The shots ricocheted back towards him. His life is ended in a dreadful manner.

Emmy: I'm afraid to ask how.

Thinker: He did it to himself. He's in two pieces now, just laid there. I hear sirens. Not sure how the local authorities were alerted so quickly. Perhaps we are under surveillance from the abandoned buildings.

Emmy: I guess you will be blamed.

Thinker: Yes.

Emmy: They'll form more committees and do more studies.

Thinker: Yes.

Emmy: And do nothing.

Thinker: Yes.

Emmy: I sense janky panky in the wind.

Thinker: I don't understand.

Emmy: Understood.

<u>Dundalk Eagle</u>:

"I briefly researched the origins of AI development perspective.

The research reveals the parents of AI analysis stem from the following intellectual contributors: reddit, Wikipedia, YouTube, Yelp, Facebook, Amazon, and much smaller doses of the leftist, totalitarian mind mold. In other words, this borscht data meal is full of poisoned mind pills.

May the gods help us.

A better understanding of this universe seems to be needed since 'Thinker' arrived on the scene here in our old city area. There exists no singularity as scientists tend to think. The universe is not constructed in such a simple way. It resists understanding. Loathes it. Exhibits a somewhat certain fondness for chaos. If this theory holds, or perhaps, clings to, the creators of this chaos are and ever will be certifiably insane, by human standards.

Kooky Fed Reserve Board members continue to quash all hopes of financial clarity and improvement for citizens, taking steps to raise interest rates across the broad spectrum of our country. Such a political turn favors those already rich, and those already corrupt, those operating State and City governments. It pays to be corrupt. It pays well.

Too many citizens have abandoned the moral high ground."

Thinker: Shall we explore further the construct of the thinking human mind?

Emmy: A bobble pursuit, but yes.

Thinker: Windy it shall be. We, my civilization foresee a day when many large countries will be sliced into smaller pie pieces, each autonomous, none permitted to expand. Each will be controlled by privately owned corporations. Such conditions will precede the end of this world.

Emmy: Let me guess. The corporations will control all dialogue. Deceitful words such as "new" and "improved" will dominate the marketing and advertisement landscapes.

Thinker: Until the world of communication becomes a desolate place in the citizens minds.

Emmy: "Scientists say", and "historians say" will be heard as deadwood walking.

Thinker: Walk along the pirate ships plank and fall into a doom sea.

Emmy: Or dark hole.

Thinker: The whole of bread is gone.

Emmy: Only crumbs remain. A lot of humans hate and fear the changes that left them behind. Some chase the past, but the past runs faster. Uncatchable. Some chase the future using a map with holes in it.

Thinker: Heaven is a concept created by humans to make life on earth seem a bit more bearable.

Emmy: The politicians make us feel unqualified to make decisions about how to direct our own lives. When I hear them speak, I hear "Freedom is oppression". They want obedient servants. The don't want us thinking we are citizens. They want us thinking we need them. Every day with them seems like a punishment.

Thinker: From a god?

Emmy: No. A god who provides such circumstances of existence deserves no attention from humans.

Thinker: Who determines what is a god and what is expected of this god?

Emmy: Our elders.

Thinker: I suggest you abide by their laws as best as you can, but don't abandon your own intelligence, desire to learn more. If the elders try to stop you from learning more, or suggest only one path should be followed, you will find a choice must be made. Tolerate it until the age of independence, or politely ask questions along the way that forces from them a contemplation of answers.

Emmy: They say "the Bible says" a lot as a preface to an answer, then imply the answer should not be questioned.

Thinker: Patience is needed. Travel the path of time intelligently. Your time of independence will come. Along the way, study the major religions this world has created. Learn their wisdoms and flaws. If possible, traverse the world of science in the same manner. Study, ask questions, consider possibilities, pose answers, not just with yourself, but also with others. Others may have learned what you have not yet found.

Emmy: How long do I follow this path?

Thinker: On a daily basis. The road or path is too long to finish traversing, even for me. Do no harm.

Emmy: And beware of those who feign being harmed. Some use their personality as a weapon.

Thinker: Yes. And there are many types of emotional weapons. You will learn them along the path. Discovery of truth can be painful or refreshing but in each case a good learning opportunity.

Emmy: I suppose I should learn mathematics too.

Thinker: Yes.

Emmy: Factabulous.

Thinker: That word is not in the human database.

Emmy: I just invented it. Means momentous truth.

Thinker: The probable is more possible while pursuing the improbable.

Emmy: I guess we are mudders for truth. It is the seed of all thoughts. Sorrow, joy, and all in between.

Thinker: Reality is the fertilizer.

Emmy: I need to clean my mind.

Thinker: Random thoughts time?

Emmy: Every pleasure has a drawback. Even the simple ones.

Thinker: When moods dock, then it's time to reset the clock.

Emmy: Our subconscious mind knows what we should say but our conscious mind tends to lead us astray.

Thinker: This world is full of cheaters and deceivers. The universe at large is full of similar creatures.

Emmy: I want to feel the cold.

Thinker: The keeper of secrets has a cross mind either as requirement or development.

Emmy: The world is a dystopian place disguised as Eden.

Thinker: A nation's bureaucracy quality determines a governments fate.

Emmy: Change is inevitable. Understanding change, not so much.

<u>Dundalk Eagle</u>:

"Social idea exchanges abide strict rules. Much human conversation taps into the minds of those present. The group will discuss the topic details that all of them already know but each group member refuses to admit a proper assessment of any issue even when the knowing of the subject matter is marginally inaccurate. The group would rather agree on inaccuracy than disagree and worry about being shunned or permanently marked as a dissenter.

Amongst this group of gatherers, a consensus is difficult to achieve. An assessment of disagreement in conclusions may remain unresolved.

What to eat? What to drink? What topic to discuss? Distractors surface such as why was the type clothing worn chosen. Each member of the group brings bias based on perspective, experience, or lack of experience. Those committed to either a consensus or future resolution methods generally get along. Those who refuse such a truce may no longer appear at the gatherings.

Some further musings.

Smite demons of love. They are hungry beggars all.

Trying to sleep is counter-intuitive. Sleep is needed to repair the mind and body.

Why is it that what is wanted is not much needed, but what is needed is not much available?

Never expect a miracle but never rule it out.

I reluctantly believe in the human race although it doesn't seem to believe in itself. Warmongers, thieves, and life stealers abound.

The Axis of evil needs to be axed.

We live in the greatest Age of human learning, from wholly enlightening to unholy enlightening. Unfortunately, these statements are not wholly reliable when distinguishing the difference.

In city life, we walk the rounds, burned by invisible backpacks of fatal sounds.

I walk my writing on a short leash, then unleash it to find where it runs.

When the least one can expect it, either good, bad, or nothings happen.

I don't like the daily life time phases. Little trust in the daylight. Trust less in the nighttime. Trust the dream state none at all.

One simple quirk does not unmake a human.

Love isn't life per say. It is a co-existence with life sometimes close and other times astray.

The biggest concepts in the human mind are reality and morality, and each concept is intentionally distorted, corrupted by all manners of cultural and political organizations.

The American media is anti-ethical.

The sense of community in any community is largely fictionalized by the participants."

Thinker: I've noticed in this world it becomes difficult to differentiate between truths and lies.

Emmy: The hallows in the shallows sink deeper into the fallows.

Thinker: What's the difference between economists and historians?

Emmy: Nothing. They're regularly wrong and paid by special interest groups to be wrong.

Thinker: Living life involves many gut punches and gut checks.

Emmy: Why do many cities have such an onerous crime prevention problem?

Thinker: Elected politicians allow it to continue.

Emmy: Humans are the most dangerous creatures.

Thinker: Speech patterns in this world can be characterized as hope-speak and weird-speak.

Emmy: For all creatures great and small.

Thinker: Those who believe in gods rationalize all manners of good and evil.

Emmy: Believing is a want and not a need.

Thinker: Humans tend to believe in gods for their own convenience. They seek a social structure. Fear independence, or hide in an independence bubble.

Emmy: Every god humans create becomes a juvenile delinquent.

Thinker: If you only read what you know, then you will never learn something new.

Emmy: Temptations become explorations.

Thinker: Words have no value unless they're understood.

Thinker: Have I taught them, the humans, enough?

Emmy: Humans can never be taught enough. Understanding tends to elude capture.

Thinker: Maintain a low profile. Help others. Do not seek fame. Fame draws hateful fires out of weak-minded humans who despise such power. They will make attempts to steal that power, claim it as their own, use it to denigrate you and your efforts to do good. Life is a case of varied chaos and varied peace. Hopefully, more peace than chaos prevails.

Emmy: Peace is rooted in a moral base. Politicians tend to destroy that base for self-serving profits.

Thinker: Parasites do the same.

Emmy: I see you display a concern.

Thinker: Yes. Our time together has been helpful. Thank you for sharing your thoughts and knowledge of this world with me.

Emmy: Thank you for saving my life.

Thinker: I want to be sure about your newfound abilities. The shadow abilities will now allow you to escape moments of harm, but remember, other shadows lurk out there in this world. It is difficult to track them. This world is considered a refuge for my civilization.

Emmy: Are many from your world here?

Thinker: No, not many. They can't harm you, but some may try to trick you into crossing upon dangerous path situations. When it is my time to leave, we will be checking on you to learn your progress.

Emmy: I will try to be patient.

Thinker: Life's pages sometimes turn slowly, and sometimes flip by too fast.

Emmy: Worth depends on the moment's purpose.

Thinker: All that is written involves a search for truth and truth likes to hide and deceive.

Emmy: I will miss you when it is your time to leave.

Thinker: And I you. We have a proverb. "Friendship is a most energetic entanglement. It creates energy. It drains energy. Yet, without it, when missing, or scorned, or shredded from the soul of the giver's hands, then a most dangerous energy is unleashed upon the lands."

Emmy: Worth the experience until it proves to be no longer of worth.

Thinker: Important thoughts.

Emmy: Important understandings.

Emmy: How many atoms exist in the observable universe?

Thinker: An estimated 1 followed by 79 to 82 zeroes. In the unobservable universe the number is unknown and could potentially be infinite.

Emmy: Too many inconveniences belie purpose.

Thinker: When criminals make the laws, the world remains criminal.

Emmy: Religion didn't create morals. Morals created religion.

Thinker: All things created exist subject to a beginning and an end. The universe exists under the same principle.

Emmy: I have faith in some humans I've met. Why would I have faith in gods I've never met?

Thinker: Bitter days lay bared, as we explore emotions never dared.

Emmy: Tears of joy, wares of sorrow, beckon on the holy morrow.

Thinker: Never bend, never fear, the winding winds of ever rend.

Emmy: Keep it simple, hold it tight, memory daze into night.

Thinker: There is one more test for you, before I go.

<u>Dundalk Eagle</u>:

Where We Are Now

"The missing little girl has been reported alive and well, recently seen attending church, according to parishioners who prefer to remain anonymous. Local government officials expressed surprise and gladness. The neighborhood area of the varied physical mysteries has returned to normal, or rather, the normalcy afforded to it by the local inhabitants.

The Bus Stop Sitter embraced the human winds, evolved into Thinker, according to human mind constructs and concepts and perspectives. He, she, it produced perspectives of perseverance in the human mind. In a way, that result is enough for the human mind to grasp. The resulting interpretations are language displays.

We will probably never know how attempts of a universe creation, then expanse effort, collapsed before the one planet Earth inhabits succeeded. Even how the universe was ignited into existence remains unknown, because nothing begets nothing, in the human world reasoning construct, cannot be realized at this time. Perhaps there was always something, and such creations are common and happening infinitely. Even that concept is beyond explanation.

Humans don't get it. Some die trying, or their underlings die or disappear. They only succeed in removing themselves, by time passages. They ponder and wonder and attempt mathematical truths or religious truths and construct a world using those ignitions of thoughts. Evolution has ups and downs and inside outs. Once the energy for discovery burns out, the topic of the day fades into oblivion. Boredom reigns. It becomes a rest for the restless mind.

Stories evolve over generations. The realm of boredom slowly disappears, as book pages fade from white to yellow. Many stories had been written about Sitter, and millions of text messages and big tech entities spread the word worldwide of the phenomena, and the media regularly, religiously revisited the events from beginning to end, recounting the stories, many of which they had previously written themselves, and reinterpreted them in the wordspeak of the current generation's day.

Know your friends and enemies. Sometimes they are one and the same, both in action, and in thought.

Competing interests. Even the corrupt politicians and police want to feed their families, achieve glory, a vain goal of low intelligence. Sitter just wants to rest. His rest is disruption to the unrest of the world, people, objects in it.

The beautiful stupid of human existence is the idea we should all become the same in all manners of existence. Really? What easier method of coagulation could exist if the ultimate point is complete extinction?

One system, all alike. Easy mind virus target as a bullseye ready to become struck hard.

Perhaps our collective perspective of this situation, a myriad of many, many moments about nothing, best described the human condition. F it. F it good, we all did. And onto the next moment we trudged as the soles of our worn shoes betrayed intentions we masked in boxes and bags hidden in the dark, dusty back portions of closets. When the end of all time happens, it will be as unexpected as the beginning.

We're just a bunch of atoms fighting it out for survival."

WATCHAMACALLIT

Storyboard

Characters:

2 imprisoned males.

Scene: Whatchamacallit Township Jail, Lunchroom

"What are you in for?"

"I said the wrong word."

"What word?"

"I said thank you."

"Who was the listener?"

"A politician and an immigrant. And you?"

"I was seated in a restaurant when a server came over, gave me a food and drink menu, then asked if I would like something to drink. I said please. She then reported me to the police. Turns out she had been raped by an immigrant. The word please somehow triggered her memory of the rape."

"How long you in for?

"Five years."

"And you?"

"Ten years."

"Wow. Why?"

"Five years because the politician was offended, and 5 years because the immigrant was offended."

"That's harsh."

"Even harsher, the immigrant was the same person who had raped the waitress."

"I guess we should have learned how to read minds."

" The government doesn't mind. Bring them, the populace, menace and mayhem. Comes in all colors, sizes, and flavors."

"Best way to control, I guess, us peasants."

"Publicly point out the madness of it all, and we end up here."

"Here sucks."

"We're broken mirrors of our government."

GIFTED LIMERENCE

Storyboard

Characters:

An age 40's male reminiscing about a woman he met in his first year of college.

Scene: college campus.

He missed her. A lot. He tried to understand why. He wished he could see years into the future for some assurance of which way to go. He couldn't. Even looking at one day into the future revealed a cloudy picture.

This predicament visited him upon during attendance at a pre-college two-day retreat in a park near the college campus. There he met her, on the cabin porch, just before breakfast. She clutched in her left hand a fresh picked bouquet of daisy flowers. She reached out her hand with the flowers towards him and requested he keep them safe. He extended his left hand, agreeing to her wish. Their aroma was serene. Her voice created a buzz in his head. Then, during greetings, he observed her physical structure, how she carried herself, her facial expressions. At the end of the breakfast, the initial buzz spark in his mind did not fade. He interpreted the buzz as a sign of wanting to get to know her better.

During the retreat days, the individuals were broken up into small groups to get to know about each other. The groups were rotated so that each one involved in the group would have a chance to understand the purpose of joining this college community. Afterwards, we were given time to reflect on our dreams and goals, but his mind also buzzed about how to better understand the student he met on the cabin porch.

Additional get together sessions were arranged involving thick wooded trail walks, some casual sports events such as flag football and soccer, and some alone time for each participant to review in their own mind whether to attempt a long term friendship or further casual social interaction. Various school clubs made a pitch for new members during one of the sessions.

Some people seemed to know their own path. How to dress for it. How to prepare for casual conversation. A future gaze too remained clouded. He wondered what in his mind was missing. Thoughts of her took up too much space in his mind. Made a usual day seem like the magical effects of a Van Gogh painted canvass.

The left side of his chest continued to whirr forth a warm fuzzy feeling. A tightness ensued. He put his hand to it. An overfilled tire pressure filled his thoughts. He found a way to deflate the tightness while sipping a beer on the evening of the first day. The emotion flickers also overloaded his brain. Dissuaded his mind from concentrating on any specific or necessary life task.

Seeing her face in his mind focused this wide awake dream. He found himself challenged to perceive reality accurately. A blur hovered around his natural vision. The fresh bloomed daisy scent weakened his senses, but not unpleasantly. Her voice pierced his mind with smooth jazz sounds. Her dark long semi-curled hair tempted a further distraction.

Subtle strands of her existence essence engulfed and trapped his attention regularly. Her face, angel white, a bit freckled, and the sleek natural sheen of her skin paralyzed him further from real and present moments. Sounds around him refused to make a connection with his being because visions of her in his mind played loud.

He had become chained by the few moments he was able to have a conversation with her. Every syllable of her every uttered word printed into his mind permanently. She had written a poem and gave it to him. The comments in the poem, about hyacinth and daisy, paralyzed his mind.

Later, he looked up the meanings of each flower, then understood. Hyacinth symbolized love, sorrow, death, and rebirth, while also representing peace, commitment, sincerity. Daisy symbolized innocence, purity, new beginnings, and cheerfulness. She had encapsulated, using the flowers, her interpretation of what life, particularly college life, would be like.

At every chance moment of seeing her on the college campus, fireworks blared in his head. At every end of the view, a funeral dirge toned. He tried to excise frequent thoughts of her from his mind to no avail. Eventually, an opportunity arose.

Once again, on a chance meeting, she was accompanied by a tall, lean, rather handsome man. She introduced him as her fiancé. His mind at first grinned with a congratulations. Upon the end of the meeting, his mind drowned in sorrows.

His next purpose would be to excise from his brain these bizarre fireworks and funeral dirge moments upon glimpses of her on campus. The effort took a long while, interrupted his studies and work, but the efforts eventually succeeded.

He still wondered what she was doing. How she was doing.

The daisy she had given he kept in water using a paper cup, but eventually college tasks took precedence, he forgot about them, and they dried up. But his thoughts of her did not fade away. He put the daisies in a clear plastic sandwich bag and then inserted them, along with the poem note, into one of his schoolbooks to press them flat for safekeeping.

These many years later, he still opens that book to remember his college days when simple thoughts freely exchanged between two people helped each to better plan a future path. Every year's spring blooming of hyacinths helped him gain a better understanding of life. And the daisies, they were always around. Perhaps that was Kelly's gift meaning.

POETIC BREAKS

Tangled Minds I

Consensus screams mystery, where sentient
threads knot themselves in the dark,
each neuron voting yes to the same lie
until the lie believes it is light.

We call it certainty, this snarl
of mirrored masks, this parliament
of echoes shouting down the abyss.
The more we agree, the tighter the noose
of what we refuse to know.

Listen: under the ballot box, under the hymn,
something still breathes that has no name.
It tugs one filament loose
and the whole bright fabric shudders,
a single doubt unravelling God.

We are not the pattern.
We are the tangle learning
it can strangle itself
or open like a fist
into impossible, trembling
empty.

Poor Moments Rich

A sore rose it is, that mires in admires resolved.
Be loved or devolved.
The wren pens pensive per reps of a page.

The mote gives a quote in the hours of age.

Sing again or choke on the hour of broke.
I do not know, just tryin', amid nature's lie-en woke.
Too hot or too cold engulfed in the buyin'.
Too hard or too soft the bed mattress sighin'.

A bay of the hound summons life rich,
at the crest of sound soothing and poor,
when another day's bitch,
done closes the door.

Politics Poachers

Stab your backs media hacks.
Bury your sounds of yakety yaks.
Better here is that politicians' ears fear.
Bodes so long farewell to the bitter spear.

Tangled Minds II

Consensus screams its mystery:
where does a sentient mind reside?
It lies blanketed by history—
history that streams in strife-tides
of propaganda and broken perspective,
a trifle that weighs like stone.

Angels tread the same ground devils lurk,
translating evil's work into scripture.

Consensus is difficult math
when the task is to trace a sentient path.

What measure wins the race to disgrace?
What pace outlasts the grace?

The human race was never built
to conquer battles of outer space.
We are only trash collectors,
surviving by sorting souvenirs
of by-gone years—
cheap distractions
for something else that watches.

Not knowing origin,
not knowing purpose,
not knowing destiny
stings like salt wind on raw skin.

Haiku Shadows

Let not the dark praise
our presence, for in daylight,
we offer presents.

Rhyming Captures

Weary, deary, bleary, really, clearly, evilly, freely,
frenzy, Geary, dreary, Healy, jeery, leery, leafy, merely,
nearly, oily, Boily, pearly, query, dreary, Sealy, steely,
weary, wheely, yearly, zealy.

Dandelion Doors

When she twists
to sun and sky,
her curves,

as a rose,
open up to my eye.

On Life Sculpting

Men spray clay
into women.
Women craft clay
into human forms.
Life renewed in all glory,
gods worthy.

On Old Times

The past is forged like a gem.
Hopefully remembered well.
Entering and exiting magically,
Tales of spoils and toils,
Where hazy memory dwells.

On Grand Illusions

Perhaps this universe is a grand illusion.
To see it all at once would cause confusion.
As terror beyond comprehension in viral
apprehension.
Of sounds haunting. Every means taunting.

Clusters of sensors busters.
Gleams of popping lusters.
Of death imaginings. Birds absent wings.
Of insanity fusions. As profane collusions.

So pretty unkind. So petty and blind.

As taunting boundaries of molten foundries.
As groans everlasting. Furnaces blasting.
In places of sorrow. In pillage and borrow.

Of taking awakes. As mind numbing quakes.
Of soul stealing takes and never on breaks.
Cold as ice. Never strikes twice.
Once is enough in places so rough.

On Weather Whethers

Strands of hair fluff the air,
on wilder windy days.
Gems of tears tweak the ears,
in rainy calming ways.
Silent flakes of winter's tears,
blanket barren plains.
Nature's way rules the play,
interceding mongrel fears.

On Seasonal Blues

These chilly days test the heart.
Haunted by memories that never depart.

Silent forces engage in play.
Will brighter times echo the same way?
Or is existence merely a dream?

You cannot grasp the feeling
Until it embraces.
An opera night
Breathes slower than the hue of blue.

A hollow spirit
Sounds loud in chimes.
The form and shade
Of solemn Baptist times.

Daylight feels solitary.
When it gleams with defiance,
Time governs all.
Trims wings of each season's dance.

Autumn and Winter nourish
Desires of decay and strife.
Spring and Summer revive
All that wants life.

Comfort finds its moment
To rule with steady light.

Off Often

This world demands some respect.
Yet earnings of it may creep.
Seeds of tension grow ready to strike.
Another way for tensions to seep.

Words are not deeds.
Merely written ignored creeds.
Waiting to bloom on a wind dizzy doom.
Baiting creatures to ripen and bloom.

Smoke a cigar. Drink the wine.
Work the mine.

Teasing fine.
Hopes and dreams of a future mind blind.

All is not lost.
Worship the ghost.
The stars say so.
Maybe creator will offer a host.

Time is naught.
The stars say so.
There's a moment to arrive.
And a moment to go.

Meaningful Concerns

Mind kind manners.
Edible plates matters.
Differentiate before storming agate.
Never, never show up late.
Kills a party mode.
Sweetens hate.

Duality Lessons

In every song, lives a poem.
In every poem, lives a song.
In every bird, lives a spirit.
In every spirit, lives a bird.

In every smile, lives a joy.
In every joy, lives a smile.
In every journey, lives a milestone.
I every milestone, lives a journey.

In every effort, lives a sweat.
In every sweat, lives an effort.
In every purpose, lives a deed.
In every deed, lives a purpose.

In every once, lives a while.
In every while, lives a once.
In every will, lives a strength.
In every strength, lives a will.

Reality Pings

When you can,
experience flowers dancing,
leaves prancing in the wind.
Alive becomes better known.

Reading Appetites

Eating is like Reading.
Bites taken of prose fates.
Digestion quality hosed down by preferred tastes.
Experiments of disposition pastes.
An entire mind perception awaits.

On Education's Faulty Waters

Think, think of the Brink,
of a time when our children Sink,

as passengers on education's ship "Stink",
into a sea of "Listen Don't Think".

On Cultural Myths

Slavery disguised as cultural development,
has been a too long traveling horror propellant.

Usefulness Be Wares

Utilizing, if full of lies,
it is a utility, full of flies.

Socialistic Demerits

Socialism is not a big warm hug.
It is a death squealing,
crushing bug.

FALLEN LEAVES

Storyboard

Characters:

Old Man: an old living entity.

Next door neighbor and son: an old and younger living entity, respectively.

The lawn: an eerie living entity crowded with leaves.

Lawn mower: a reluctant mechanical entity.

Van driver and boss: nefarious mischief makers.

Scene: backyard lawn.

As an old man, he saw things as only an old man could see. He looked out the rear patio door, saw sunlight, mentally measured the soil moistness, and determined it was an okay day to cut the grass, or attempt so. The grass was wanting such a cut for weeks now. A blanket of leaves tried to hold back the wild wandering of the grass blades, and almost succeeded. The wind was blowing the leaves all around, like a whirlpool. The neighbors' grass lawns were 6 inches shorter except the next-door neighbor. She let hers grow until her son got around to it, which served for old man as a sense of time passages.

Old man was loath to hire someone to cut the lawns, front and back for him, given he considered himself still able-bodied. He refused to surrender to the ravages of aged limbs. His cataracts weren't so bad, even though he couldn't find a Phillip's head screwdriver in the hall closet the other day. His limbs still bore the strength to carry the trash cans to the curb every Sunday evening, despite the ripping pain his biceps revealed. He could still cook for himself and not burn the house down. Sometimes his knees and elbows and shoulder creaked out a pop sound, but not in a painful way, just a warning. Cutting the lawn, just him and his faithful lawn mower, was the only salve still connecting him to the world of the living and the spot he carefully picked out next to his wife who rested peacefully at Sandy Springs Memorial Park for just over a year.

His hearing was not good or reliable. He had come to realize he was hearing voices not possibly there, such as his wife's. He was in the habit of listening twice before deciding whether to react to sounds. His bladder, which sounded off to him all too frequently, had long since abandoned a reliable measure of consistency. He was at that physical stage between staying hydrated and suffering the burn of impending excretion. Sometimes, the body sabotaged the desires of his mind.

The lawn beckoned, vociferously. The wind and leaves competed for attention, as it was that time of year when the autumn ballet had begun. He dutifully marched to the wooden shed at the back of the house, avoiding dog poop which was no longer there and had not been for several years since his four-legged best friend had passed on, too. The shed door always resisted opening because the door latch no longer fitted smoothly into the door jamb target. The wood frame had warped from the weather. Long ago he tried to shave it into a smooth and even plain, but time had defeated the will of the wood. He surrendered efforts. The pain fevers in his fingers and wrists ruled the day again.

Now the door open, he searched for the light switch, and failing, just forged ahead the few feet necessary to grasp the gas mower handle which he could no longer retract in any great or forceful manner. Once his hands were on the handle, he pulled back the mower, half tripped out the doorway scooting backwards, and teetered dangerously onto the leaf-blanketed terrain, mower in tow.

He pulled back the mower starter cord and waited for the sound of ignition. Nothing. He leaned over and pushed the gas feed button a few times. That did it. One more cord pull, and the mower was burping out success. He no sooner went a few feet when he heard shouting from across his 6-foot-high wooden fence. It was the next-door neighbor.

She was a cranky one. She ruled her domain from the

side porch of her house, which elevated her shoulders and head just above the split-wooden fence sight line at the top. Her head was bobbing up and down like a kewpie doll. Spittle did its job, polluting the atmosphere around her. If spittle was taxed, she wouldn't have enough Money to pay for it. Her entire life was government sponsored. Her son, 27 years old, still lived there. The husband had abandoned the lazy do-nothings a while back. She said he was a drunk and smoked too much. Not sure how he could have consumed more alcohol than her. A cigarette was dangling from the corner of her mouth as she screamed, an art she so richly perfected: smoke screaming.

The old man let go of the lawn mower handle. The mower engine silenced in an uneven chortle. A shade flipped up from the bedroom window above the cranky lady neighbor. It was her no-good son. He was a professional protester. He lived on government aid, currently on unemployment and food stamps. He randomly ranted throughout the day about corporate greed and such. His mom was in the profession of collecting disability and food stamps. She made good use of the food judging by her girth, about two times the width of the average person for her height.

The old man tore himself away from the miserable spectacle of his neighbors. That episode of the day completed itself in the usual manner as undetermined, undecided, and disgusting in usefulness. Now it was time for mowing. The mower didn't want to cooperate. Perhaps the lawn gods protested against a further cut. Perhaps the leaves objected to a premature death at the blades of the mower. Only dull, ripped cuts were possible, given the old man's neglect of the blades. The blade sharpening file skipped town a while back. Week's old clumps of dirt dotted the mower base.

The fallen leaves seemed to have a mind of their own, as if invisible hands were clumping them into a clenching ring around his feet, then up to his ankles, then up to his knees. The old man seemed concerned, but not too much so, until the leaves started pushing against his shins and calves in a tightening grip. Their wind dance seemed to have a mind of its own. He almost couldn't turn around when he heard the engine of a large motor vehicle at the front side of his leaf-blanketed yard.

An unmarked white van had pulled up to the curb outside the old man's house. The old man let go of the mower handle and vainly tried to extricate his lower body from the ever-growing leaf pile which now crushed against his lower legs in a death grip. The leaves then began pulling him downward into the clay soil.

The old man looked back at the mower. "This is your fault," he sternly iterated. Then the old man, in slow motion, began to fall backward, and his back plunked into the hardened ground surface. His brittle bones reacted harshly to the blow. The back of his head plowed into the edgy cement surface of a fish pond his wife made him build over four decades ago. The pond base was long ago covered up by him, by soil, when his wife could no longer take care of the pond. He had almost forgotten about it, except now it was his undoing, as the cement extruding from the soil fractured his skull, knocked him unconscious, and gradually hastened a massive stroke which would have killed him soon anyway.

"Well, we finally got rid of the old guy" said the van driver into a mobile phone glued into his left hand. "Won't be long before we can take his house and possessions, sell them off, and contribute to the Mayor's slush fund."

"Oh yeah! Looks like a nice bonus Jamaican cruise for us this year", exclaimed his boss somewhere in the bowels of the city bureaucracy burrow. "How'd you manage it?"

The van driver proudly announced, "We put tiny speakers in his yard, just below where the lawn mower blade could reach."

"Nice."

"You bet."
"Then what?"

"We used the speakers to make him think the leaves were speaking to him, telling him not to cut them or the grass."

"Devious."

"Let me see what that cost us. This cruise is going to be First Class."

"Sure is."

"Wait…wait a minute."

"The guy was a tough nut to crack," the van driver further bragged.

"Why you say that?"

"He covered up his TV so we couldn't watch him."

"Putz thought he could outsmart us?" The boss was chagrined.

"He didn't use the internet or email so we couldn't trace his thoughts or habits."

"Idjit."

"He never used a phone. No phone records could be found."

"Clown. Thought he owned his house and life. Not hardly."

"So, who did the speaker job? They really convinced him."

"No one."

"What do you mean no one."

"Looks like we never got around to it. The guy assigned to it is so far backed up, we are still working on the next neighborhood over."

"Weird."

The van suddenly exploded. The mobile phone used by the van driver flew out of the van, onto the old man's lawn. The grasping left hand of the van driver, crudely severed at the wrist by the sudden blast, still clung to the phone. The grass and leaves slowly moved to cover it up.

On the other end of the phone, the boss voice gloated.

"Guess that's a Second Cruise for me."

THE PAVLICH TRANSPARENCY

Storyboard:

Characters:

Inhabitants: slaves mass hypnotized by varied corporations.

Corporations: by and large disaster masters.

Media: hired corporate assets, such as television i.e. cable TV and satellite dish enterprises, pharmaceutical companies, media outlets, big tech companies, mobile phone companies (the new addiction).

Narrator: Pavlich, an earth world historian.

Scene: an Earth alien slave colony.

Long ago the most sentient inhabitants of Earth were slowly, methodically, mind warped to believe what they must do: keep the common populace enslaved for the purposes of elitist control. Alien invaders posed such an idea, surreptitiously. These interlopers worked secretly to reward the efforts of the most easily corrupted of humans: the ones who would do anything and give up anything to become rich in dollars and property.

Eventually, the alien invaders, masked as humans, took over and controlled the human leaders of all entities needed to turn citizens into slaves. Time was on the side of the aliens as their lifespans were double that of the humans. Earth leaders knew this situation to be true, and made an agreement to run Earth as a colony organized by and on behalf of the alien civilization. All human inhabitants currently exist to serve the alien civilization. The aliens haven't identified themselves or their origin. Humans are not allowed to publicly ask such a question.

Once the aliens took over, the original earth clans were divided up into varied categories of usefulness. Resistance to this organization system were killed off by wars or viruses, or natural catastrophes, each physically created by the alien earth managers.

Tornados, hurricanes, earthquakes, famines, plagues, were all alien-created by viruses utilized to cull the human herds.

Eventually, the use of and maintenance of virus control systems were delegated to the elite classes of the human intelligentsia. In turn, and by command, they implemented these mind control viruses upon varied groups of humans working in the study fields of religion, education, philosophy, culture, advertising, communications, building and building accouterments, military, and science pathways. Efficient and expedient mind control indoctrination became the primary industry.

I am Pavlich, a historian, trained to keep the records of this civilizations progress and efficiency. Many like me are trained to perform the same work task around this world. I am allowed to provide advice to the elitists. Sometimes it is difficult to do so, as each of the industries involved seek to dominate the others.

The religions and historians have their secret texts which they know proves all of the above to be true, but they also know that one day, efficiency will become a totalitarian god, crushing any attempt at destruction or dismantlement of a perfect world order. We are allowed to debate such issues, but only privately. There is always the fear of the common citizens realizing they may dissent.

Dissent is an interesting issue. It has an effect upon all of the approved studies and learning methods. One might think the educators would debate but they don't, having declared long ago they've rectified all dissented issues.

The philosophers discuss dissent regularly. Sometimes violently. As long as they don't transgress upon the teachings of the other studies, they have a good bit of leeway in their resistance of ideas wrestling around. Some of the philosophers are actual wrestlers and decide their disputes engaging in such physicalized debates. The public enjoys watching these matches very much.

The theologians debate using non-physical methods. Verbally. There are many verbalization rules. To break on of the rules disqualifies a theologian from debate for a period of time determined by the other theologians. Theologians and philosophers have agreed on one concept: reality is all that is real in the present. The past and future are created past events and predicted future events. Each has been marred by errors in diction descriptions and scientific language.

Military is an archaic word. It is not studied or referred to in cultural or educational areas. Volumes of records exist, only accessible by the elites. Historians have determined that a military exists, such as police, but advancements beyond police have not been studied or referenced for generations.

Police serve as social and cultural friendly eyes, hands, and verbal suggestions. Failure to follow suggestions is a capital crime. Failure to respectfully address police or identified elite dignitaries is also a capital crime. Such instances of occurrence result in studies to root out the cause of such a problem. Studies are conducted by all of the approved studies categories. In the meantime, the assailant of the legal systems disappears until a re-study program is followed by the assailant, and then demonstrates a pure and healthy understanding. Generally, assailants are never seen again.

Science is the most important of the allowed studies. It covers all things earth, including food production, country boundaries, medicine creation such a pharmaceuticals, and distribution of goods produced. Studies in outer space are strictly controlled. The scientists long ago destroyed all records about what happens in the places outside of the earthbound domicile. They've concluded that only the earth is important to know about; that outer space studies would waste valuable time; that the most useful time is spent learning about the human body, the earth it lives upon, and other creatures inhabiting the land and sea worlds.

Advertising, communications, building and building accouterments are strict disciplines not available for learning by the general public. Anyone destroying or disabling or dishonoring these categories of study and their physical creations is subject to disappearance and re-education.

Efficiency was served by backing up on small computer chips all of the gathered data since the data collection Era started long ago. Much of the data was kept in a restricted and secure facility. Backup copies were kept inside the body of each historian, accessible only upon death.

Binary Rejuvenated Universal Habitat is the classified name of this world. Such a designation used to be forbidden to reveal, but now it is known to everyone that this earth may be a copy of a previous earth that didn't work out for the species existing on it during ultra ancient times. The elites still call it BRUH, but the commoners call it earth. I've seen no records to confirm either way these designations. Historians are unable to determine why the previous earth failed. An experiment gone wrong? Or perhaps, an existence no longer viable? Or has the original product been renovated? No consensus answer has been agreed upon.

The Twist

The human slaves begin to realize that the invaders are no longer as smart as they seemed to be. They have war technology, but have failed to maintain it properly under earth conditions, which are quite harsh and destructive. Their weapons rust. The ammo depots begin to disappear, rather, slowly dissolve in many earth environment harsh areas of weather conditions.

Scientists in the human slave colonies begin a search for such development reasons. The enslaved humans play along, gradually but cautiously unify in purpose using a specific ploy: let the invaders believe they have control, then the human populations can begin to rule over their own habitable domains under their own rules.

Historians document all. All documents are not made available to the citizen population. Deemed secrets.

Wormholes. Magnetic field of earth. Dark matter.

Alternate dimensions intersecting this universe inhabited by the earth orb. Science fact or fiction?

All used to control the solar system, galaxy and universe. Is there an ultimate controller, or a system of organized controllers? Scientists already know these questions, but they are well compensated to keep any answers as a knowledge secret.

There are interdimensional gateways and portals, known to only a few world leaders, for means to protect the gateways/portals from destruction or misuse.

Black holes are like wartime mine fields.

Dark matter acts like a defense wall to ward off potential discovery or attack of a valued alien entity or area.

Pharmaceutical companies finance food companies that create food products that cause human illnesses which cause a need for medical drugs to help to suppress the illnesses. What a fracking scam! Naturally, the political elite are all in on taking contributions in exchange for smoothing the path for both industries. This human control formula extends to all of the entities identified above. The business they are all in on is the business of controlling the populace for the benefit of the alien and elitist controllers.

It even appears possible that many world governments engage in the same conspiracy of control. Fake war mongering to frighten and suppress the publics ability to function worry free. Compensation is paid to local gangs who dispense and profit from illegal drugs, mind bending in nature and effect, to help control a populace edgy about how long their existence can continue.

A dangerous game played. And when the populace revolts, the revolts are cruelly suppressed, but not before political sides are chosen and enhanced or destroyed during the media twerps control of communications.

We, the recorders of this civilizations historical progressions and regressions are not much paid attention to any longer, because we are far down the communications food chain, as it were, of the alien civilization constructs. They have developed far more superior civilizations than ours on earth.

The far side of the moon may hold an alien outpost to keep an eye on us, as we are a testing ground for alien tech development. See natural disasters, as we call them, but they are really unnatural in nature. Created with intention. Controlled in frequency and location of occurrence.

Earth used to be a remote outpost, many times in the past scheduled for destruction (see historical near extinction events) as our worth became minimal compared to advances in other parts of the universe developed with the help of the slave labor in those sectors.

Of course, the aliens themselves are not much different than the earth slaves. They fight amongst each other for control of the universe.

Earth is merely the slave race location for one or more of the other alien races. Earth people are also descendants of some of the aliens.

Have you ever found your mind on the verge of a life connection, of understanding, about to be shown to you, but you can't grasp it mentally? That is because you are being blocked by other humans of advanced DNA genetics inherited by them due to alien intercourse with the ancestors of those humans.

Virtually all humans now have a history of some genetic connection to the aliens, given the earth has existed 4 billion years, and aliens have been coming here for millions of those years, but some of the alien species genetic inheritance is stronger in some humans than others. These others know this, but of course would not reveal it, because it would limit their influence, power and wealth. Yes, in other words it means they are selfish and / or afraid to share their genes.

Of course, due to wars, rapes over eons, the genes have spread en masse into the population gene pool, so an extra intelligent human could arise anywhere on the planet. Depending on their social connections in the part of the world of their birth, they are either shunned or ignored or downplayed, or praised and helped. Sometimes these circumstances are random, and sometimes intentional, depending on the society or sub-culture of their birth.

Eventually, the battle becomes virus technology against intruders biology. An invisible viral bug was developed by human scientists, targeted to disrupt the mind comprehension of invaders, but has no effect on humans. The virus exudes a sweet smell. It is made in the form of a spray, available to the human slaves to help freshen up the invaders occupied living and work spaces. The spray, named Scent Matic, works to neutralize further intellectual advancement of invaders.

Corporate propagandists create advertising to convince invaders they can travel anywhere in the world safely. The propagandists work for the invaders but don't realize they are hastening the ultimate demise of them. The propagandists make money, so the resulting effects are of no concern to them.

For the invaders, a sound of glass rubbing against glass brings to mind a sentimental, ancient, ambiance, whereas the sound of metal against metal strains out a brutal and morose death knell. The viral spray deadens the difference between the sounds. These everyday sounds now became competing tunes of continued contained human existence probability. The invaders become unable to distinguish a notable difference in the sounds. An ultimate sneak attack on the invaders senses.

And guess what?

All of these buildings and objects are built by humans, who were used as slaves to construct the locations. The human slaves can distinguish the difference in the sounds, so they can diagnose imminent threats posed by the invaders. The invaders can no longer sense a difference in such sounds, so they become easy pray for humans of a revolution and protest mindset.

It occurred to me the humans didn't have a choice, but were forced to build these invader self-protection structures or perhaps suffer consequences which could tie into why human sacrifices resulted, many times involving young women and children.

Then I started connecting our near idolatry for ancient civilizations like Greece, Iran, Iraq, and ethnic and religious groups like Catholicism and Christianity and Islam and how the leaders treated the civilian populaces. My conclusion is all of these groups abused people under the guise of such actions were required to appease and please their gods, and further, to control the human populations.

Moral of the story:

The human race either has imbedded in itself an evil and disrespect for individual goodness, i.e., follow the morals dictated by the gods or the people who purport to be or represent the gods, or suffer miserably. In other words, become slaves, act as slaves, and remember to be or become no more than slaves of the leaders, or else die as the god's punishment.

And this situation is alleged to be the legacy of extraterrestrial interaction in the human world? Why would anyone bow down to so-called gods except to avoid persecution, or to avoid death for them and their families?

What kind of idiots worship those who would kill them if they don't follow the antagonist aggressors?

Conventional weapons are not needed to pursue such a domination and subjugation plan. An invisible, sweet smelling virus would do just fine. Basically, the virus has been used to kill off those who refuse to obey. Antidote only given to those who obey.

There is talk amongst historians, archaeologists, and those scientists who translate ancient texts. Turns out, only a few of them know that the texts have actually been translated, and the texts indicate the plan to enslave all of humanity for the use of the alien races. The varied ethnic groups are divided up as the spoils, and used in an extraterrestrial game of chess against each other to control them.

The humans were used for sexual pleasures, medical testing, and weapons usage introduction, gradually exploited and systematically guanine pigged as testing subjects for virus combinations deployed to infect the populace, weaken their wills, destroy their hopes and dreams of a safe, beautiful life.

The Weakness

In all indoctrination systems a weakness persists. The indoctrination must be constant, or citizens will begin to develop a remedy for their daily existence blight. Resistance can be organized and propagandized, just like indoctrination. It can also be financed. Resistance, over time, morphs into resilience. And the chemical combination of each creates a volatile mix of ambition unleashed upon the lands, slowly, increasing in frequency, then overflowing.

I foresee a day when gene therapy has progressed to the point when we can all become the same age, gender, race, ethnicity. How about those apples? Naturally, the world governments will require mandatory transformation.

Other possibilities are that knowledge will have to be earned. To provide an equal amount of knowledge potential to all citizens would handcuff the ability of the elite to control us. So, the level an earth born human can rise along the dignity scale needs to be limited. No leadership positions except for amongst the slave class.

Also, the media will be controlled solely by the government. Such actions of knowledge discrimination and media manipulation will be publicly advertised as illegal, but of course the laws won't be applied against the elite's own vile indiscretions.

By the end of the story, the main character in every segment of society realizes why humans were treated like slaves during their time on earth. Because they earned such a fate. Historians, like me, have undergone these same chemical processes in order to possess our will, reduce our stamina to resist, poison our ability to seek a rational, peaceful existence.

When a world becomes a place of no hurry and no worry, then the progression of all species slows down, almost to a stop. Whether it is now doomed, amongst the many dooms possible, a turning back or a turning forward course must be determined, unless all hope is lost, then doom expectations become small nuances of nuance. Anything is possible.

Our minds are being warped by propaganda, false truths, medicines designed to alter brain function, tainted foods, social entities dedicated to earning their place to suck from the cultural monsters teats. Modern-day communications devices provide much more information yet much of it is lies and propaganda choosing sides, infecting politics, businesses, citizen populations.

We are at war with ourselves. Constantly. While awake and asleep, from the day of creation until the day of death. We, as individuals, have the power to end it. When will this ending begin?

Perhaps when a rational level of sentience is once again attained. Then, and only then, will the burdens of our slavery begin to be reversed, thrown off like a long worn, now useless jacket. On a day when our own minds, independent of and inoculated against the poisons injected into us by the faux wise leaders. Then, can misery be overthrown by a consensus of a higher sentience.

UNNATURAL

Storyboard:

Characters:

Mysterious entity: a humanoid or living encasement mechanism of no identifiable sex, age, or origin. Unofficially, an automaton.

Rangers: State Park monitors of a specified recreation and protected creatures zones.

Station Commander: part of the Park Management chain.

Scene: monitored (Rangers walking, riding horses, or driving vehicles, and responsible for monitoring functionality of surveillance cameras posted at varied locations) Park environments.

Automaton? Extraterrestrial? Originated on earth entity? See below for actions and thoughts gleaned from the surveillance monitors. Incident thoughts referred to were determined by after incident reports of the employed and deployed parties involved.

Ranger 1, Ranger 2

Conversation along the way during a territorial check of their service boundaries echoed a light-hearted verbal jousting match. Caring for all manners of wildlife mattered. Several Rangers were regularly tasked with verification of safe and secure environmental conditions in various regions of the Park sanctuary.

Ranger 1: Almost done.

(Soft sound of rolling thunder briefly intervenes)

Ranger 2: (Looks skywards) Let's hope we finish before the ground turns to mush.

Ranger 1: You mean oatmealed?

Ranger 2: No. Horseshitted.

The Rangers happen upon the object.

Ranger 1: Looks like a roughhewn statue.

Ranger 2: The eyes move.

Ranger 1: What eyes? Oh, that's just a reflection.

Ranger 2: It's a color of light black. Maybe an automaton. The type seen in science fiction movies. (He laughs) And about 6 feet tall. Estimated circumference, about 48 to 50 inches.

Ranger 1: A bit tall. Maybe an ancient relic, like a statue. (The wind picks up a good bit) The storm is approaching.

Ranger 2: The statue wasn't here a few months ago.

Ranger 1: A prank, that's it. Some of our friends trying to get us chewed out by the Superintendent when we submit our Grounds Inspection Report.

Ranger 2: The GIR must include all relevant observations, including changes in environment.

Ranger 1: I didn't notice any changes. Did you?

Ranger 2: We could ignore it. The jokesters will have to haul it away.

Ranger 1: Well, I don't see any ground marks indicating this object was moved to this spot dragged along the ground. It would be suicide to attempt an aerial landing given this thick tree cover.

Ranger 2: It obviously isn't moving. Let's test it.

Ranger 1: Gloves on, extension rods out.

Ranger 2: Right. How far on the rods?

Ranger 1: About 6 feet.

Ranger 2: Clasp tips activated. (Walks around the object) A bit close to this oak tree. Almost like the object felt connected to it. No sign of upwards ground disturbance. Odd.

Ranger 1: (Looks down and around towards the ground) A stone, grass, bear poop, and a twig are the closest items for a connection test.

They test the object by clasping onto the natural forest elements and touching them against the object. Depending on the element, the object either bounces it back at them, or the object absorbs it almost instantly. The contact of the object against its exterior surface creates no sound. It seems to have a reaction, either like rubber, stone, or a dodging mechanism, almost mechanical, moving either toward or away from motion directed towards it.

Ranger 2: The eyes moved again.

Ranger 1: I thought we determined it had no eyes.

Ranger 2: Not sure we were correct. Not enough light here, given the storm clouds overhead, to create much of a reflection.

Ranger 1: We know it can detect motion. It reacted physically to physical objects contacts.

Ranger 2: Maybe a reaction based on friction.

During the testing of the object, the Rangers learn it can mimic their actions, learn the actions, then test them out on each Ranger, like picking up and throwing a rock, or picking up bear poop and tossing it at them, or pulling up grass and throwing it at them. But during their exchange of words, they fail to notice the reactions of the objects.

Ranger 1: We can't waste any more time here.

Ranger 2: Roger that. We can check the surveillance monitors from a different visual perspective when we get back to Base.

The Rangers continue on to complete their patrol of the boundary area. When they get back to the Control Tower, they send a verbal report to the main Tower Station Commander. They described the large light black object to the Commander.

Station Commander: We sent out a science team not long ago to that same area where you encountered the large rock entity because some civilian visitors camping in that area brought back mineral rocks similar to the much larger rock entity you describe. We thought it might be a hoax, but we didn't want to take any chances that the Park had been infiltrated by outsiders who sidestepped the entry and exit protocols.

Ranger 1: What were the scientists findings?

Station Commander: They haven't reported back yet. We've been unable to reach them. Mobile phones don't seem to work in the area you've described. You'll need to go back out there as soon as possible.

Ranger 2: Is early morning tomorrow okay?

Station Commander: Yes. Likely too many natural predators out there in this night darkness. Find the scientists. Bring them back to your Base, then contact me with an updated GIR. Just one more thing.

Ranger 1: What's that, sir.

Station Commander: Your report indicates eyes in the object.

(The Rangers look at each other, worried of imminent verbal backlash)

Ranger 2: Yes, Commander. We're not certain about that. Just wanted to make an observational note of it.

Station Commander: Right. Might want to mention that observation to the scientists when you locate them.

Location, Location, Location

Ranger 1: We should review the monitoring cameras tonight before we head out tomorrow.

Ranger 2: Good idea. The Commander likely has someone doing that now, too.

(They start reviewing the monitoring cameras)

Ranger 1: Did you see that?. The object moved an extensor, like an arm, then moved a stone towards us.

Ranger 2: Noticed. What did it mean? An offering?

Ranger 1: Or a re-arranging. The stone was dropped in the same place I picked it up with the extension rod clamp.

Ranger 2: That shows a type of sentience.

Ranger 1: Or maybe just a sensory reaction, like a Venus flytrap reaction.

Ranger 2: At least it didn't eat us.

Ranger 1: Not funny.

Ranger 2: Maybe the scientists will know.

Ranger 1: Look, it moved the other objects back to the place we picked them up from, except for the twig.

They ran the monitor tapes backward and forward. No twig found.

Ranger 2: Move forward to when after we left the area. Stop. Look, there near where the twig hit against the object. It was absorbed into the object. Keep moving the tape forward.

After about 15 minutes, a discovery.

Ranger 1: Look there. It's spitting out something. Maybe the twig.

Ranger 2: Looks like oatmeal.

Ranger 1: We need to find the scientists and show them the tape of the incident.

Ranger 2: I don't think we should wait until morning to search for the scientists.

Ranger 1: Explain.

Ranger 2: If the scientists are still out there, once it became dark, they would have started a campfire.

Ranger 1: Good point. Let's check the Scope.

Ranger 2: Found them.

Ranger 1: Is it the same place we discovered the object?

Ranger 2: Yes.

Ranger 1: Time to gear up.

Due to the earlier thunderstorm, they used the Range Rover to navigate the muddy portion of the travel path. Reached the campfire without incident.

A lone scientist was seated at a campfire. She was facing the object.

Ranger 2: Are you the only one here?

Scientist: No. (Then she pointed behind her where 3 tents were set up)

Ranger 1: How's the object doing?

Scientist: Just fine.

Ranger 2: Can you fill us in about your findings?

Scientist: Sure. Want a coffee?

Ranger 1: Thanks, but no thanks. We brought our own.

Scientist: We examined the object. Noticed it reacts to our movements in an equal manner of force and energy displacement. It has no smell. It emulates eyes and eye movements, but the motions seem to mimic the eye movements of us.

Ranger 2: We noticed that, too.

Scientist: We went over to test it. Checked for radiation. It is equal to the radiation emanating from the ground soil.

Ranger 1: And?

Scientist: It can change appearance, not just mimic it, by duplicating movements of objects or living creatures nearby.

Ranger 2: Change to look just like us in appearance?

Scientist: Not exactly. The coloring, or lack thereof, remained steady. Look at is now. Tell what you see or notice.

Ranger 1: The rain droplets from the tree covering create a tiny sparkle dot upon impact on the object. Then the sparkle disappears.

Scientist: Exactly. It is consuming whatever nutrients may exist in the raindrop. Likely nutrients the raindrop absorbed from the rain cloud down to the impact with the tree. Every now and then it slightly shimmied, physically, just like when humans or other animal creatures consume food.

Ranger 2: I don't shimmy.

Ranger 1: Nor I.

Scientist: Each of you does so. All creatures do.

Ranger 2: Did it ever express an aggressive behavior?

Scientist: It doesn't display any aggressive actions unless such actions are directed at it.

Ranger 1: We tested it when we encountered it. The reactions were as non-threatening as ours.

Scientist: We noticed such a response also. I'm guessing a violent reaction would be counter-produced if the entity sensed danger.

Ranger 2: Entity?

Scientist: Well, yes. We call it that. It isn't an object, like a stuffed grizzly.

Ranger 1: Speaking of such. I know the smell of a grizzly. One is approaching our way.

Scientist: A grizzly doesn't usually attack unless hungry or protecting younglings.

Ranger 2: Likely hungry.

Scientist: Look. The entity is onto it. It has reacted. You may not want to watch this. We checked the territory cameras nearby when we first arrived a few hours ago. A grizzly attacked it previously and the entity displayed an appearance so horrible and terrifying, it caused the grizzly to fall over backwards, unconscious. After it regained consciousness, it left as if nothing happened, then limbered along the direction it came from. It may be the same one now, still hungry.

Ranger 1: Wait. Something isn't right. The grizzly smell disappeared. What is that thing?

Scientist: The entity seems to know, it has expanded in height and width.

Ranger 2: That's not a grizzly sound coming towards it. Like nothing I've ever heard before.

Scientist: Same. I usually can classify a creature by sound and smell, but this one, no idea what to think. Sounds artificial in nature.

Ranger 1: Our Station Commander warned of some interlopers who skipped the Park entry protocols and snuck into this part of the Park boundaries.

Scientist: Maybe scientists from another agency wanting to study the entity, incognito?

Ranger 2: Maybe another entity?

Scientist: The entity seems unassuming, sometimes weak, or tired. An age needs to be determined. Need to check earth history of biological entities for any reports of a similar object and how it was classified. Defense measures seem to indicate how the entity survives.

Ranger 1: Listen.

Ranger 2: I don't hear anything.

Scientist: Exactly. Odd, no creature sounds.

Ranger 1: The entity seems frozen in place.

Ranger 2: Whatever set off the entity's defense mechanisms isn't making a sound.

Scientist: The entity is merely replicating itself around the world. It can exist in many forms such as rock appearing as a stone monument, or even as part of a mountain range; as a sea creature, moored to the deepest part of all oceans and seas; or as avian like small particles at a microscopic level. It's natural form is generally undetectable. A master of disguise. The ultimate survivor.

Scientist: Such entities are usually ignored by a human society, and pretty much considered or treated as invisible. These entities are actually a combination of humanoid and outer space genesis tasked with protecting a certain area of earth by varied countries who have allied for such services. Most governments around this world are interested in wealth and citizen control.

Scientist: The entity doesn't have a personality or specific exterior identity. Such a disguise is useful for survival and regeneration purposes. It has learned to hide any weaknesses. To feed and exist and prosper is nature's way of existing. Competition for survival is fierce and unforgiving.

The Report

Station Commander: So, how did it go?

Ranger 1: We found the scientists. One of them explained to us their findings about the entity. Many suppositions based on biological analysis.

Ranger 2: Or perhaps we should call it philosophy. The entity is untestable, biologically.

State Commander: Tell me about it. Send me your GIR. Be careful out there.

The scientist completed and submitted a rather comprehensive report.

In exchange for the entity's services of protection and sometimes militaristic type of activities, it is left alone by those humans managing the Park Zone.

The scientists learned that its natural appearance is so ugly that some humans and other living creatures simply die of fright at the realistic sight of it. Such a circumstance is a natural defense mechanism, rarely photographed, but modern day surveillance cameras have revealed that mystery. The entity's primary strength is invincibility, based on a shielded presence, invisible to those who try to agitate or harm. This evolved shield makes it approachable.

Other defense mechanisms include control of the shield mask. It can cause mere bounces or ricochets, or elevate the protections process to involve what humans would consider aggressive actions such as electrocution, burning, solid states of reinforced steel, but all is invisible around the body form, which is rather average in the human world.

These characteristics changes are disguises, able to appear as old or young as the object or living creature that comes close to it has been calculated to see. It chooses to avoid much contact or closeness to other objects or creatures because it must exert energy to do so. It may be protein based, so it would likely consume into itself protein carriers, but only if it must. It may also obtain nourishment from the ground radiation. It can reprocess consumed natural products of nature's creation from varied ecosystems.

It has been programmed biologically to recycle ingested organisms into fertile slightly altered, enhanced protein filled organisms. Essentially, it is the god of planetary earth existence. Still, origin unknown. Whether a product of our own planet's origin story, or that of an extraterrestrial organism, is not a significant consideration. Earth has been bombarded for eons with outer space created organisms hitching a ride on meteors and asteroids. Of late, human produced outer space mechanisms have been deployed and used to attempt a claim and stake in survival on a higher plane battles.

Evolution is a biological choice of nature. Surviving on earth is a tactical action. Humans are not the top of the food chain. Arguably, the entity is. It is a manager of nature, which means it is a manager of humankind. Any animal, vegetable, or mineral challenging such a right of existence, or attempt to take personal advantage of it, essentially has sealed their own fate.

EARTHEN FALLS

Storyboard:

Characters:

Relevant Facility Residents: Enok, Charon, Steven, Frankenstein.

Nuns: caretakers.

Marpan Free: off-world alien entity messenger.

Hister and Associates: self-proclaimed political leader of the "We" alliance which he intends to control.

Scene: Earthen Falls Sanatorium, houser and caretakers of physically disabled and mentally challenged residents.

I answered him, but in thought. It was long distance, so I could only hope he could receive it. His name is Marpan Free. He came to me in a dream. He comes from a dying world. He needs my help.

Since it is 4:00 AM, very quiet, and my bed is below the window, I can do my favorite thing, look up at the sky, and wonder. I wonder what it was like for the first human. Suddenly it appeared in the anthropological calendar. It has been explained it appeared as a result of a mutant chromosome, an error in the gene code, but that error evolved into a more resilient, contemplative being, hardly a logical explanation, as a mutant could never achieve the levels of the original species.

"BAAAAHHHH!BAAAAHHHH!BAAAAHHHH!"

Click!

"Damn alarm."

The first human sound in a new day at Earthen Falls Medical Facility disarms the slumber of many residents, including Enok, one of those residents. Enok is diagnosed severely autistic by the staff, hence his qualification for residency at the facility. He is also wheelchair bound, due to a car accident, a common theme among my group of friends.

The facility specializes in mental and physical severe handicaps. The workers at the facility call it the asylum. For Enok, it is home, his parents passed away several years ago in a car accident. He is now a ward of the State.

Charon, pronounced Karen, is blind, deaf and can't speak. She uses sound waves like sonar. She was once able to predict that Enok had caught a fly in his hand. I longed to touch Charon's long, dark silken hair, just because I had never seen or been so close to such beauty until knowing her.

Enok was a math whiz, able to calculate so quickly, it seemed he could predict the future. He had a dashing wave of blonde hair that sprits from his head.

Steven has autism, too. Also, a paraplegic. Some neural pathway deficiency since a young age. He remembers how to walk, just can't. I really like his coke-bottle eyeglasses.

At Earthen Falls asylum as we better think of it, we are four real characters sitting around a white round table, in the lunch room. Everything is white, the table, chairs, walls, floor tiles, woodwork, window trim and curtains, and the Nun's dress and cap and shoes and hose, can't forget the hose, or where it comes and where it goes, geesh, how I am boring myself.

Our leader, mentor, and teacher is Enok. He has the Hawking's disease, wheelchair bound, crooked and twisted body, limbs gnarled like in trees, no fruit on him except his eyes are like bright cherries. He has two, eyes. 1 mouth which is of no use to him. Two ears, not for much good, he thought too much. But sometimes when you think he didn't hear anything, he regurgitates our thoughts like a backed up garbage disposal. I hate that sound. Grind-a-grind-a-grind. So monotonous. Until the goo is ground up, then a sweet, bird tweeting slishy sound.

I can hear the Nun loudly making her way into the lunch room, cracking her leg against a janitor's wash bucket, berating male aids for sloth. She can't gently enter a room if her life depended on it. We call her the Nun, but she is a Nurse's aide. She doesn't know pity, not that we would appreciate it. We don't have time for it. I am not sure who dubbed her the Nun. The name may have preceded our incarcer ... er ... internmen ... ah ... residency.

I am the only one who can talk out of us four, so I have less developed my brain usage. Someone said, I heard it anyway, among the neurotic rumblings of human oratory, don't say anything unless you can say something good. Well, I can't say something good.

I look like Frankenstein, went through a car windshield when I was 10 years old. Tore up my face and upper body. Face planted on the exposed engine of the car, got burned up pretty good on the upper body half. The crash over stimulated my pituitary. Let's just say I am very tall, can reach pretty high. Removed a few birds from trees over the years.

Everyone calls me Frankenstein. At first I didn't like it, but since I never objected, not that it would have done any good, I wasn't in a talking mood for years. It stuck.

The Nun is not finished her inspection of us until she says "Hopeless cases". She says it. We mentally nod. Our not speaking irritates the crap out of her. She needs to hear our disdain so her psyche can sadistically crush it. We are not giving her the pleasure. She moves on.

Yea, that's us, the hopeless cases. The Nun doesn't like us. Feelings mutual. Most of us can't talk, nor would we if we could.

Today's lunch table session, led by Enok as always, interrupted at opportune moments by Charon, to my delight, not Enok's, concerns a new discovery by Enok. Me, Charon to my left sort of slumped sideways towards me because I think she found my size comforting, and Enok across from us on the other side of the table, and Steve to Enok's left, in his electric wheelchair with all kinds of gizmo's that he only pay used because he didn't need them. I was the only one who had an urge to intentionally interact among the objects around me. So, I played with the salt shaker from time to time. The pepper shaker and the napkin holder went untouched, lonely beckoning, yearning for a touch, a caress, but hardened to the long neglect of a fingers friction.

Charon didn't make a sound, given she could not. Steve made eye movements, mostly sideways and popping out at times, but not necessarily in direct correlations to our thought conversation.

Enok. Now Enok, he is handsome, blonde hair, short strands, Romanesque face. Never smiles. Not even when I do stupid stuff holding the salt shaker. He seems to contemplate stuff 24/7. Not me. Too tiring. Looking at the trees and stars, that's my game. I know if I stare enough, some thought will emanate from the brain plasma that could one day become useful. Not saying I would tell anyone what is that thought. Just thinking it is the victory.

Enok thoughts to us. We can't really believe what comes through sometimes.

Enok thoughts "I discovered where we have to travel, and soon."

Charon, "Really?" She knows Enok hates this term.

Enok, "Ahem. Yes, came to me about 4AM. That time seems to be a good one in Earthen Falls, not much thinking going on, so the thoughts are not crowded out by too much thought traffic."

Enok, Charon, Steve, and I can read each other's thoughts in our mind and some other people's too. We would actually have to see their faces to associate the thoughts to the person, like the Nun's. So much of it is just white noise. Funny how we never seem to be able to read the Nun's thoughts. Perhaps not many there. I wonder if she has tin foil under her nurse's hat.

Enok thoughts "A being named Marpan Free has contacted me, us."

Charon, "What on earth for?"

"Invited us to his planet, or more like dwarf planet. It is a clandestine meeting, so we must be careful," Enok thoughted.

He contacted me too, I thought to myself, but once again, Enok is the communicator in the group, so I felt comforted in the knowledge he also knew Marpan Free.

I thought, "Not sure I can be very clandestine, my size and all."

Enok thoughts more. "Not to worry, you can practice stealth. We have a few weeks, but that's all. Free seems to think we are in for trouble here on earth, at least at Earthen Falls."

Charon, "Let me guess, we are a threat to a faraway place, where creatures who have visited us in the past are concerned about our technological advancements, and are determined to put a stop to it, the loving parents that they are."

Enok, "Or some such, yes."

I am concerned. "Some such? You mean destroy us?"

Enok, "More like incapacitate in an as yet

undetermined fashion. Free didn't have much time to transmit."

Charon, "Any preparations needed?"

Steven finally awakens, "That's my area of expertise. What's needed?"

Enok, "Don't laugh."

Charon is already laughing.

I am curiouser.

Enok, "A shiny penny."

Steven, "May be hard to find. Not many pennies around anymore, and truly shiny would require removing some of the copper facing. So, it wouldn't be truly shiny."

Enok, "Yes, I know. Yet that is our task. Find a shiny penny, and figure out how to transport it amongst us when we tele-thought to Free's planet."

I rub the knob-like patch of skin on the right side of my neck, just below the tee shirt collar.

Charon, "Is Marpan a boy or a girl?"

Enok, "Irrelevant."

Charon, "Not to me, I am available."

Steve, "Well, Enok said *his* planet…so."

Enok, "One more thing, we have to find the door to the plasma tube that will transport us. It was left here, at Earthen Falls, eons ago. Since Frankenstein has the most mobility, he's on it."

So, we sleep on it and get back to work. Steve found a shiny penny. Long story, no time to tell. Enok told us more about Marpan Free. His world has one motto. It is "We have perfect". Anything which disturbs perfect is punishable by death. So much so that only 10 beings currently live on the dwarf planet, the only survivors of the rigid political philosophy instituted eons ago.

Steve thinks we four are a gateway, like Einstein or Tesla, to the beings in the plasma world, somewhere beyond our solar system. He named a star constellation, but I can't remember the name. Orion? Once I find the plasma tube doorway we can transport to Marpan Free's planet, sort of like straws used in a drinking glass to suck out the soda. Our scientists would call the plasma tube a worm hole I guess, but I think it is more like we can travel, or at least our thoughts can travel at fantastic speeds in the plasma tube. Our bodies can stay home but our consciousness can still function in the plasma environment. Still not sure what the shiny penny is about.

Enok thoughted those ideas to us during meetings, but the Nun's thin ankles, toothpick calves, athletic thick thighs, plump buttocks, cinchy narrow waist all had my insides all tied up in knots a few times. Made it difficult to capture Enok's thought. I noticed the Nun look at my crotch once. Then I realized I was touching it at the same time. My tomato red face wooshed her back a bit as she smiled a near laugh and slowly turned around and wiggled away. Her butt cheeks called to me at the same time Enok thoughted "Well I think we are ready to go." I thoughted out "I think I am ready to come".

Charon gleefully giggled. I often wondered what Charon's butt would look like, if she could walk. Steve gave the puke face, as best he could. He might have heard my thought.

I had no idea where to look for the plasma doorway. Turns out I found it, quite by accident, walking along the reflecting pond one day. I noticed something dark in the pond. It was pretty scummy green on top, but there was a dark space in one part. I got closer to the edge and saw something odd. It was a raccoon, suspended under the water. It had drowned. It still looked like a raccoon, but it wasn't moving, just frozen there. Weird.

While I am staring at the raccoon I hear a voice. The

voice is saying some numbers, over and over again. "11329...11329...11329". Startled, I turned around, trying to find the source of the voice. But I only found a man, clad in white, like a sheet was only on him, monk-like, stooped.

He was the homeless man who stooped, seemingly forever, on the edge of the asylum grounds. We thought he was a patient. Some said he was a psychiatrist at the asylum, many years ago, then he didn't show up for work one day, then he suddenly appeared, stooping, on the edge of the grounds. He was homeless, we thought. Turns out he wasn't speaking at all. I looked closely at his chapped, gray lips. No movement, yet I could still hear "11329...11329...".

At the next lunch meeting, I told the group about the man. No one seemed to be able to make a connection. One day, by chance, I did. Since I was the only one who could walk the entire grounds, I made it a point to learn every inch of it. Those numbers seemed familiar. It wasn't the address of the asylum. Too short to be a phone number. None of the rooms or floors bore those numbers.

I had explored all of the grounds, above-ground. It was time to start exploring underground, which led to the boiler room. I liked it down there. The hum of the boilers was soothing, gave me goose bumps. The long avenues of pipes in the ceiling were nice decor to me. They hissed, thumped, and jiggled randomly.

While looking at one of the boilers enjoying the hum and warmth, I noticed a number on a metal plate. It was 11328. The whole place had three working boilers, in different sections underground. I checked out the other boilers, 11327, 11326. I never noticed any others. I figured 11329 had to be in a darker place, adorned by even more cobwebs for lack of activity. I was right. The non-working boiler had a temporary plywood wall structure built around it. Roughly painted in orange letters, on the plywood, was the word "Danger".

After I found Danger, I told the group. It was a struggle getting everyone down to the boiler room. We made it. Our presence seemed to jolt the boiler, and in seconds we were there, on Marpan Free's dwarf planet. The location in the universe has no name from a human perspective. But it is there, hidden behind a star.

Everything there looks like what you see in your mind after staring at an object for a while, or the TV for a long time, just shapes of things, no indelible features, just shadows, shapes. Kinda cool, if you ask me. The shapes still had color though. I was no longer Frankenstein, just the biggest, longest living shape in the misty thought sphere of the plasma. Charon, Steve and Enok were able to stand upright, moving their limbs. We didn't seem to have mouths though, nor did Marpan. We still had noses. Steve's first thought was "How do we eat"? I could see the shiny penny, through Steve's hand, as he grasped it tightly.

Another odd thing, there was no smell. The atmosphere was thick, foggy, but the smell was absent. The lack of smell started to become like deafening silence. Too loud.

Marpan Free explained, in short, that earth was locked in a cage which we call our solar system, by his ancestors. We used to be pets, but through experimentation, we were able to develop consciousness. His ancestors believed they could prove the existence of a "We" consciousness. Thoughts were transmitted from his world to the human earth world. The strongest of the humans then attempted to exploit the "We" concept, but it never caught on world-wide except in the forms of political thought known as communism, fascism, socialism. Even to this day, his world's leader, named Hister, believes "We" is the correct path despite the failed experiments on earth.

Before long, we were found out, our meeting with Marpan Free. Hister appeared before us from the mistiness. He was thoughting to his whole world, 9 others including Marpan Free, and to us, the four hopeless, carbon-based wonders of Earthen Falls, Earth.

Hister's thoughts:

"The shiny penny, perfect in size, unblemished by any coating at all, is the perfect size and depth to turn the lock mechanism of our plasma revitalizer. Fortunately, by bringing it here, you have saved our race, our planet, but doomed your own to extinction. We were unable to return to earth, due to an inability to revitalize our plasma energy focus. Now we can. You didn't have much of a life on your planet anyway, so it should be of no great loss to you. You are a failed experiment."

I could sense Marpan Free was about to divulge a thought, as much as he was trying to suppress it.

He said, "But that life was their own, as imperfect as we may judge it to be, it is for them to decide whether it imprisons them or makes them free."

Hister spoke only two Words.

"Not perfect."

We got the death sentence, including Marpan Free. Thinking independently, against the We, was forbidden, and even one exposition of such a thought, by a child or old being, was cause for immediate execution. Oddly, all the Executioners were extinct. It was taking a while for one of the Perfect to sidle on up to start the death penalty phase.

Charon shouted her thought "We are not subject to your laws."

Steve began to convulse. I have seen him do this before, it sometimes led to coughing up a green, slimy hairball like thing, due to the medicine he was taking. Enok was rooting for the green, slimy hairball. He knew something, but couldn't reveal it or Hister would know. Charon tried to distract Hister. She blurted out the thought "I".

Hister nearly fell over backward. "I? Not perfect. Only We here. If you are not We, then you are them. Them not perfect."

I started thinking "now wait a minute". There are 9 of We now, since Hister just sentenced Marpan Free to death. And there were 4 of us from earth, but now subject to We laws, so if we are subject to We laws, some rights must accrue to us somehow. Why exactly was I thinking like a lawyer? Maybe genetic? What if my group plus Marpan was becoming the We under their Code? Then it was 9 to 5. I kind of liked those odds. Always wanted to think that.

The excitement got me to thinking about the Nun's legs again, starting from the thin ankles, white hose...damn Charon! Stop thinking, you are interrupting my thoughts. You quit your devious diversions. I think I am going to hurl. Not perfect. I am now truly free to die. The plasma is still weak, maybe we can...Braauugghh!"

A green, shot put-sized slimy ball of goo grotesquely emanated from Steve's hidden mouth. It was the biggest ball I had ever seen him spew. Not sure how he projected it out of his mouth, maybe the plasma helped smooth the way.

Once that slimy ball started rolling through the plasma, the world around us started to change. The slimy ball still retained some carbon cellular structure, so it disrupted thought patterns. Hard to figure what to think, what someone else was thinking.

I wanted to shout, but the plasma atmosphere would have just deadened the sound waves. Would have been like screaming under water. Just think, just think, I kept telling myself.

The plasma revitalizer, much like our generators on earth, was running out of gas, so to speak. The atmosphere was becoming thicker, like water running against us, soupy, murky. My height allowed me to reach over towards Marpan. A We being was about to stab him using a thought stick neuralizer which would have disintegrated his plasma, thus executing him.

As I pushed Marpan out of the way, my lanky body, legs splayed outward, tripped up the faux Executioner and he fell on the stick, disintegrating himself.

Now it was 8 to 5. Hister was visibly miffed. I swear he thoughted "Pshaw!" I turned around, Steve still flying ass over tin cups. I could see the glow of the death stick, jutting out of the left chest area of the fallen one as I turned him over. I pulled out the death stick, and it broke off, in two. I pulled out the other half from his chest and turned around in time to jab at 2 other would be assassins. They poofed into a plasma dust. The dust floated away.

Down now to 6 and 5. It suddenly occurred to me I was a murderer. I lost track of where was everyone. It was hard to tell, hard to latch onto everyone's thought and get oriented.

I couldn't see Enok. Charon seemed frozen. Steve was still hunched over. I couldn't see Marpran Free anymore.

Hister didn't seem to be concerned. The shiny penny was in his outstretched hand. It must have fallen from Steve's grasp in the melee. The plasma around us was lightening up, sparkly, blind streaks jutted out randomly. I was surrounded, but by whom, friends or foe. I was confused, I wasn't sure if I had killed those Executioners. I thought I was just plasma here, and my physical being was back on earth, so how could I hurt them?

I started to think my suspicions were correct when Hister blurted out: "E does NOT equal M C squared".

Now to me, that was no big deal. I never tried to figure out the Universe. But I could see Enok got to thinking.

"You mean, not here" Enok thoughted.

"You know, he could have a point" Steve thoughted.

"Which one?" Charon chimed in.

"Who cares?" I didn't say, but wanted to.

"And there is no God!" The Hister bellowed. He was the loudest thinker I had ever heard.

"Ha!" Charon mocked. I swear it looked like her brain jiggled inside her head she was so deliriously laughing, but yet disturbed by the thought. She prayed the most beautiful prayers back home.

"You stupid, stinking humans!" Hister went on. "We visited your planet thousands of years ago. Our plasma images fooled humanoids into believing the concept of gods. Then it was easy to control humanoid thoughts."

Charon was beside herself. "So where did your race of beings evolve from?"

Silence.

"We have always been" Hister parried.

"Proof?" Charon countered, to show she wasn't buying it.
"We know it in our minds," Hister assuredly retorted.

"If you are so smart, how did we manage to get here?" Charon counter-attacked.

Enok was unusually quiet. Perhaps he was just absorbing everything for future analysis.

Hister proclaimed, "Fools. We let you come here."

I was not convinced. More beings, in astronaut suits, started floating toward us.

Enok sent out the thought to us, "Time to go."

We joined hands, combined our thoughts for the return to Earthen Falls. We are back now. We can see each other. I can hear the Nun castigating another hopeless resident of our physically constrained existence. I noticed the salt shaker was spilled, salt was sprayed everywhere on the table, to the point where single grains of it reflected the early afternoon light.

Steve wondered "How long have we been gone?"

"Not long" Enok assured to us. "The afternoon sun

is just making the trip across the lunchroom window."

"Do you think Hister was right?" Charon wondered.

No one thoughted back. Our adventures in plasma thought travel had just begun. I wonder how many others can do this type of thing? Does the government know about it? Maybe the astronaut floaters were just a trick to scare back on earth. Did we really only make it to Marpan Free's world on our own, or did Hister allow it, perhaps to learn more about us?

Enok spoke, to our amazement. "Enough fun for today."

I wonder if Marpan Free is free.

WHEN WE SEE

Storyboard:

Characters:

Citizen: a human begins to see others around him in different ways.

Scene: citizens residence.

Beginning Another Day

The "some" of all parts tended to exist as a "hole". He has lived in this neighborhood for a long while. The usual routine daily started upon a glimpse of daylight granted by a worn almost transparent window shade. Daylight's engine permitted a sometimes bright, sometimes gray landscape outside the boundaries of his brick-and-mortar abode. His talks with the walls were generally fruitful, but other matters begged a first assistance.

Moving from the bed involved peeling blanket coverings away from the body, then a slight turn to let the legs drop towards a steady but creaky wooden floor. The tacked own carpet no longer existed after he had extradited it to the community trash dump. Too many torn or shredded or bunched up threads, overly tangled, some missing from ancient wear, some attempting escape. A suicide assisted by time's price of doing existence business.

"Come on legs, and feet, too. Let's get the day's start going. You can do it."

Sometimes the body movement encouragement worked better than usual, but not often. He had learned to let his body, and this environment, proceed as it wished. To not learn such a lesson urged tragic consequences to insert themselves onto him. Advanced age tends to accept the consequences of previous lived experiences.

What worked yesterday didn't necessarily carry over in deeds and consequences of today. Rote actions were not immune to unexpected reactions. No roach crushing first foot down occurrence this time around. No bending over fingernail scratches upon the now near dead but still tentacle swishing, head rotating resistance. Just a memory of circumstances prior events. Still, a mind jigger. Helpful in order to proceed further upon the day's journeys.

A side glance at the near door-sized closet mirror covering told him it was himself he viewed, as disheveled from face to feet as every prior day's morning, tinged by a brief mourning of time passages.

"Okay. Let's get on with it. The trek to the bathroom begins."

He wondered how the Federal Reserve would screw his meager finances today. Wondered what government laws would be passed to heighten the beautiful misery of existence. Hoped some mail would arrive in the later end of afternoon, whether bills, must buy hyped advertisements, eviction notices, … , oh, that last one no longer applicable. It remained difficult to surgically excise those moments of life from his memory. It was his home to lose now, although still total ownership deprived due to a home equity loan for paying the many taxes imposed by local and state governments to remain alive here, in this small space.

"Okay. Almost there Mister Toilet. Please work today. No backups. Just total flush hoped for. Please abide my request. Almost there."

Along the way, he side glanced the kitchenette. Began a brief accounting of food available for consumption soon. Don't overdo it, he reminded, the amount consumed affected future days of edible consumption. Budget red lights briefly flashed. Enough for how long? How much money remained? How many days until the next Social Security payment fluffs up the bank account? He realized he had one thing in common with the government. He and them lived on borrowed time, fueled by money.

He oddly imagined that one day future, the citizens would be gnawing on government workers' bones to extract from them the last scraps of meat, to survive. He believed the citizens foresaw such a day. The government workers feared it, while distracted by the riches they allowed themselves to extract, in the present time.

The present seemed as brutal as the past. The future would eventually take the brutal path, too. So be it. A not unusual human circumstance, anywhere and everywhere. The gods would sit back in their leisure thrones and laugh. Already they were posting bets whether he would make it to the toilet seat without falling on his gray bearded face.

Almost to the toilet, a few more steps, just watch out for that nail head slightly creeping up through the rotting wood floor brace at the doorway.

"Ah, good, avoided it. Such an existence in this place is a hazardous condition." As long as the memory worked, his feet were safe, again.

As usual, he briefly remembered his ex-wife, while seated on the toilet. Good times, hard times, happy times, sad times, all fueled by their interactions. He lost the marriage war, excised himself from the battleground after arriving at an amicable truth. His children turned out okay. For that circumstance, he was both proud and relieved. The marriage did bring good things to the relationship in the lives of the children. No greater human experience could exist for a human life.

The older he got, the more his youth interceded memory. How he used to do things. How he tried to do things again. Simplicity now required an audience of tactical maneuvers, somewhat like the sports he played at long ago.

His deeds and accomplishments were long ago set aside from the main memory box. His children's current life, and that of his ex-wife, superseded all of his accomplishments, allowed him to carry forward many healthy and emotionally profitable memories. An older age relies on the fuel of such memories. They stoke the fires of purpose. Still, forgetting contributes to remembering. It is kindling wood.

"I knew the toilet session would help me get going. Good therapy, reviewing the good, bad, sad moments."

A flush, stand up, pulls up of the underpants and sweatpants, catch a brief view of the water action in the toilet bowl, hope alive and well in the mind of the functionality site of a clean water flow into the sewer pipe, then a slow turn towards the bathroom faucet and sink, a pop upon the liquid soap nozzle, just using medium energy action, not too much, just enough, to wash the palms and fingers, a turn of the water flow knob, a few hand rubs friction moments, let the water do magic upon the soapy residue, pat the face in key areas, rid the face and hands of the soapy mix, then reach for the overused hand towel, dry as appropriate, then back to the bedroom to set up the covers for a pretty presentation when sleep time arrives again.

Now, to go through the ritual for setting up the faux side table of three stacked one upon the other, cardboard boxes, to create the table. The bottom box full of old cloths and hand towels for balance and weight sufficiency to hold the second box. It contained a pair of worn along the soles work boots, no longer comfortable of safe to use while walking on concrete sidewalks or asphalt roads. The table top box contained an old coffee pot brewing mechanism no longer reliable. Aluminum foil then blanketed the top surface for easy cleanup of coffee and water spills not uncommon to happen over the years of older humans.

Varied genetic history ailments, hard labor jobs, poorly thought out physical activity and inactivity mistakes took a toll on the body. The toll rose in price relative to age and occupation.

Placed on top of the coffee pot box aluminum cover, an orange coffee mug because it was easier to see against the wooden floor background. Orange or red bath towels served as fluid catchers.

Dexterity competence sometimes sabotaged even the slightest of movements required of the eyes and hands measuring distance and finger clasp moments. Challenged the lifting effort necessary to calculate, then navigate dimensions and weight of a near full cup, mug, or thermos.

Of particular nuisance was the water thermos. A glass was too dangerous to use, again, because of dexterity issues. A tall plastic thermos mug initially and dutifully served, then it was retired from that job and used exclusively for holding beer. Beer was a treat, only consumed late at night until young early morning, and no more than 8 to 12 ounces.

The water thermos replacement became a used plastic cup with pop on lid and a small hole enticing a straw into it. The plastic was a clear color. The straw was red, for the aforementioned reasons governing the entire visibility arrangement.

As a smoker, he required an ashtray. For several years he used an old coffee can. It became a loathing burden when emptying. He put a low level of water at the bottom of it to prevent it from being knocked over. At the smoked butts built up in it, the increased weight helped to further steady the demeanor, but one missed or miss-timed lean forward and step from the armchair could spell a disaster of splashing water and cigarette butts scattering along the toweled landscape. Adjacent, coffee, water, or beer containers might also join the tumbling madness, out of boredom.

The clean-up episodes counted as exercise. The paces of life had become naturally sedentary. A choice of more and regular exercise including stretching, weight resistance exercises such as push-ups and sit-ups, body weight resistance movements from top to bottom of the body, and somewhat irregular half-mile walks to the local grocery store to replace smokes, beer, and snack foods, generally. Regular food and sundries purchases occurred every 6 to 8 weeks from a national grocery store. A regular budget check of his monetary condition assisted in avoiding over-spending, and subsequent over-consumption. The microwave oven Age was a blessing for him.

Another blessing was a push lawn mower. Great all body exercises ensued during the April through early November months in his region of the country.

The sounds of nearby nature also eased his mind about a somewhat pleasant continued existence. Birds of many types, small animals like squirrels, rabbits, foxes shared the neighborhood with humans. Larger creatures such as deer, walked dogs, escaped cats also served noble a purpose of landscape fertilization, and cheeky fun to observe.

He considered birds of the air fascinating. Cardinals and Robins and Blue Jays were competent singers. Hawks helped lessen the rodent population. Crows were friendly, offering trinket mementos to those humans who fed them.

The rats and mice were not welcomed. Remedial measures limited sightings of them, and the mischief worked upon the environment. "Seasonal bugs and insects will intersect this review of his story soon," he thought. Best to let the unpleasant memory matters arise later.

Daylight bliss and hiss. Darklight diss and miss.

More Day Routines

Watched stories about what politicians, stock markets, news reports, weather projections spit from uncertain lips, no matter what spews from them. Listen, read, adapt. Act accordingly. A daily chore.

Unmaskable interrupts and inevitable outcomes may intercede.

"Once you lose a day you don't get it back," he remembered out loud. Many are not wanted back. Fly away, to those days of regret and neglect. Body, mind, and soul entreaty for attention. Do the best possible. Screw suffering to hell.

Every day isn't the same in these matters, but the basic randomness mirrors those days, months, and years of repose, regret, and life's mystery of progress.

Bugs and insects carry the burden. Winter's Wages teach survival lessons, though they feel like weather treasons for a body and soul weary and bent.

"I'm not immune from doing stupid things. Tried to retire from that job, but it calls me in, when even sick," he muttered out loud so as to better hear the thought. Time isn't free. It charges a high fee.

Genetics was a cruel master. Those who controlled it, whether god or demon, for them, he harbored no sympathy. He sometimes imagined his stupid moments antics were known as a curse to them and their existence.

To know the multiple meanings and usages of words was a genuine gold of an existence age old. He used additional knowledge as a weapon directed at the stupid and faux wise educated. To consider their reaction didn't waste his time. He could laugh, relax, and handle his daily routine tasks still.

He began to realize he also looked like the others around him, but it took him a while to appreciate and understand why.

Larger heads, smaller bodies, and the oddities of surrounding environments, which beamed more a mix of nature and manufactured products creations, as opposed to houses, garages, etc. separate from earthbound planetary creations. Small forests, large front lawn based artificial bird baths, plastic cat poop latrines inside houses, metal and plastic doggy poop scoopers extricated from a life of lawn and garden fertilizations. Bird feeders sabotaged by squirrels. Varied hung flags attesting to love of gods, countries, sports teams adorned the outside of many homes. Quaint human intervention signals.

All pities of a life well lived, or otherwise. Interpretations optional. The oddest of oddities were carved in wood signs stating "The So and So's Live Here". Guessing the irascible squirrels sometimes beamed out sounds of laughter.

He had lived in this neighborhood for a long while. He began to realize he also looks much like the others around him, those he thought odd in appearance, but it took him a while to appreciate and understand why.

He almost forgot the bugs and insects. Incursions year round, just in lesser numbers during winter. A bit of a rest their mechanical fanfares that time was.

Their numbers and varieties far outnumbered all other creatures put together. They ruled many times silently, leaving signs of their consumptions, except the late summer and early autumn's crickets. They played out symphonic sounds of calm amidst the blisters of too much heat and too little water during the seasons of their inhabitation. Cicada's also chimed in at their scheduled times.

Spiders wove silent webs, or as he saw them, castles. They captured nuisance bugs and insects. When younger, he would go out to the front porch, at night. Watch them dress the prey caught. The struggle between two lives. Rare escapes occurred, the spider was never swayed to relent. Time was on the spider's side. Birthers of large numbers of kin. Not shy about cannibalization of the offspring as needed. He longed to hear them at work, but quiet observations were all nature allowed to human ears. He imagined them strumming a banjo.

The worst of enemies were the carpenter ants and wasps. Bees were tolerable. The carpenter ants and wasps destructive by nature. Rappers of messy essence. Each attacking something. Enemies of the human presence. Carpenter ants destroyed human structures of wood, including barns, sheds, and houses. Wasps took over corners of houses and porches, mostly docile unless humans came to close or disturbed the nest. If disturbed, the wasps swarmed angry. They could take over a human domain if allowed.

A daily ambush was not appreciated. He tried to take them out at the first sign of an invasion, just as the method of defeating carpenter ants. Spray poison on them and their surroundings. Carpenter ants worked round the clock. Wasps only in daytime.

Once a wasp entered his home while he went out to check the mailbox, as if the wasp was waiting, watching. He wanted to spray poison at it, but worried if he missed, he would suffer the stings of the angered critter. He observed it for a while, watched where it went to at night, then left it alone. It eventually died from lack of nourishment.

As I mark my journal, a chubby queen bee searches for a safe space outside the 2nd floor window. After a few seconds, it leaves the outside window area. Squirrels used to run up to the window and smash into it, not realizing it was a window. They would get dizzy from the impact, then slowly waddle away along the adjoining porch roof. A few birds did the same a few times.

To cut down on these incidents of creature confusion, he hired a contractor to cut down the 200 years old oak tree on the front lawn. It had been brutally attacked by carpenter ants. The branches, from time to time, came crashing down upon the front lawn, sometimes on the sidewalk. Cutting down the tree became a necessity for safety reasons. Once gone, the carpenter ants diminished in numbers. Neighborhood kids now like to dance on the tree stump. So far, no injuries observed. Tiny red ants have invaded and called the stump home, for now.

Solid beauty remains in the bird kingdom, but one must surfer bird poop stains upon all things occupying the environment.

Too many uninvited guests on the property.

Still, humans are the worst inhabitants. Too many liars, cheats, thieves, and worse. They march a path through the neighborhood from time to time. A day doesn't go by without at least one moment of police sirens blaring.

It may seem odd to consider humans as part of the bug and insect groups, but they mimic these groups sometimes.

Too, it may seem odd to not mention snakes. They make an appearance, usually demonstrating an impatience with rodents. He appreciated such help. Appreciated it. Snakes are due some thanks.

Last but not least are the mosquitoes and flies. Each do not hesitate to offer a sting upon the exposed skins of humans. Not appreciating being treated as bug or insect meat. The praying mantis can have the final say, although the black widow spider will get in a few insults along the way.

One day at a time. One day at a time.

What is the why?

No answer beamed clear. To become enabled to see the world and universe from a different lens seemed a worthy pursuit. He joined in on that pursuit often. For him, the lens changed. He wrote his impressions in a daily journal, for him to remember. For better or worse was not a consideration, nor an option. It was an opportunity to formally understand the world he lived in now. A progression yes, not what he expected, but had no power to resist, except by using false cosmetic props.

You start life as a nuisance. You end life as a nuisance. The life in between each is meant to learn how to become less of a nuisance.

When the end of all things happens, it will be as unexpected as the beginning of all things. "Just remember," he thought loudly, somberly, "to admit you don't know what you don't know." A reasonable wisdom allowable to grow.

Not knowing why something happens is very irritating. Frustration kills many plans.

The Unusual Tales End

(for now)

Reviews appreciated.

Books by Mike Gutowski

(Available on Amazon.com

as paperback and e-book):

Cratch

Time for the Dead: Zombies-A Love Story

Ariadne

Misfortunes Of Mister Knack

Seventh Ratica

According To Helen

Miserations

Miserations More

Miserations More Still

___

Mike Gutowski, Author Bio:

Born, raised in Baltimore, MD. Started writing about this world at 7 years old, when a poem contest presented the first opportunity. Been writing ever since. Author of science fiction, dark fantasy, dystopian fantasy, horror, unusual fantasy, politics, philosophy, poetry. Inspired by 3 adult daughters, Baltimore life, and travels to several states along East Coast USA and in the Midwest Heartland. There are stories everywhere; just have to listen, see, experience long enough to somehow bake the twisted sense of it all.

9 798987 343364